LIGHTS IN THE DISTANCE

Short Stories

Susan Millar DuMars

Doire Press

First published in December 2010.

Doire Press
Aille, Inverin
Co. Galway
www.doirepress.com

Editing: Lisa Frank & John Walsh
Cover design & layout: Lisa Frank
Cover artwork: *Center City* by Donald DuMars
Author photo: Kevin Higgins

Printed by Clódóirí Lurgan Teo.
Indreabhán, Co. na Gaillimhe

Copyright © Susan Millar DuMars / Doire Press

ISBN 978-1-907682-03-2

All rights reserved. No part of this publication may be reproduced or transmitted in any form or by any means. This book is sold subject to the usual trade conditions.

Published with the assistance of Galway City Council.

ACKNOWLEDGMENTS

Acknowledgments are due to the editors of the following publications in which versions of some of these stories have previously appeared: *Crannóg, Criterion, The Cúirt Journal, Northwords Magazine, The Stinging Fly, The Sunday Tribune, West 47, Windows Authors and Artists Anthology 2004*. Acknowledgment is also due to the Arts Council of Ireland for the 2005 Literature Bursary awarded to the author, and to Lapwing Publications, which published a mini-collection, *American Girls* (2007), containing versions of many of these works.

I'm personally grateful to my father Donald DuMars, my brother Robert DuMars, Liam Duffy, Dennis Greig, Catherine Hunter, Maura Kennedy, Noel Monahan and Heather Brett, and to the members of The Writers' Keep for all their help and support. Finally, a big thank you to my husband Kevin, and to John and Lisa of Doire Press for their belief in these stories and in me.

CONTENTS

Belfast	7
Knowing My Brother	27
Potential	37
Stupid Slim-Neck Audrey Hepburn Dreams	47
Eve	52
The Man without a Team	62
Earth-Bound People	70
Fondly	78
Grace	82
Blood Loss	95
Live Nude Girls	103
Everyone's Mother	107
Lennon and McCartney	120

for my dad

BELFAST

'SUNDAY ROAST?'

'And peas and potatoes. Yorkshire pud.'

'I thought we'd just get a take-away.'

'Nah. Sunday dinner. Proper.' He banged the oven door shut.

'When did you do all this?' She surveyed her kitchen. Potato peels and mucky counters, the bin needed emptying.

'This morning. Couldn't sleep.' He rubbed his hands together. 'Gorgeous bit of meat. Can't wait to slice into that.'

'Should've taken one of my tablets. You'd have slept then.'

He turned away from her. Checked the back door was locked. 'Tablets, stuff the tablets. Wanted to DO something. You might show some gratitude.' Went off down the hall.

'Oh, I'm grateful,' she said to his back. 'Up to my eyes grateful. Ready to go?'

'Yes.'

'Did you check the back door?'

In the car he listened to the match while she fixed her face. Her lips looked like bruised plums when she finished. He said nothing. A squirt of the perfume their Alison had given her for Christmas. Smelled like armpits to him. Lately he'd noticed everything smelled either clean or spoiled. Perfume and the shopping centre, spoiled. Wet grass and cooking meat, clean. He couldn't explain it and wouldn't try. He thought of his roast and grinned.

'You're looking pleased with yourself.'

'Michael Owen scored.'

'M-m-m. So who's going to eat this proper Sunday dinner? Just the two of us?'

'Thought we'd ask Evie back with us. Seeing as Sammy's away.'

'Alright.'

'And we might ask Jimmy.'

'Jimmy? You're asking Jimmy?'

'Why not?'

She thought of the full ashtrays. Her well-chewed pencil and crossword puzzle book on the arm of her chair. The light as it would be then, slanting and expiring in the overcrowded sitting room. Jimmy like a giant in a mouse hole, crossing and uncrossing his powerful legs, his face soft with sweat, the smell of him a secret signal. While Evie snuffled into her hankie. And he, her husband, in his crimson slippers, turning on all the lamps. She couldn't stand it. 'Jimmy won't want to come,' she said, folding her hands. 'He doesn't like a big meal after the club.'

'He would if someone offered it. Have a heart. He's got no one.'

She said nothing.

He found a space easily enough. The 3:30 news came on. *The death toll in Madrid has risen again,* the announcer began. She said a rapid silent prayer while he turned the radio off. They paused together for a moment before climbing out of the car.

The cold. Brick row-houses squatting in the March wind and withering, wash-day sun. He was around the corner and ringing the bell before she'd got over the dazzle. 'Open up Albert, it's freezing out here,' he shouted at the one-way glass. Albert opened the door of the white, unmarked, one-storey building. Just inside, a video game flashed red and purple like a throbbing vein.

'Hiya Mr Glass, Mrs Glass, just the two of yous? Right. C'mon in.' Albert consulted his clipboard, made some notes. All Albert's movements looked important. They allowed him that. Allowed him his too-long hair, his fat yellow mustache. He'd seen his girlfriend, that pretty Boyd girl, through the breast cancer last year. He was a good lad.

The club had no windows. In the main room the green-shaded lights made an endless smoke and brass twilight in which she felt at home. She stood straighter, returned the greetings of a few regulars. Strode through the sea of mostly empty tables to their usual booth. Her husband would get the drinks. She felt the room rearrange itself around her and smiled. She liked herself here. Liked him too. They were who they were, only better: Rose and Georgie Glass.

The place was going downhill, he thought. Time was they'd have had a packed house on a Sunday. Laughter, a card game, music on the hi-fi. Instead there was horse racing on the telly, that spotty lad Rodney behind the bar, a dozen people quiet over their pints. Felt like a waiting room. And at his age, Jesus! Only one thing left to wait for. 'And a packet of cheese and onion when you're ready there, Son.' Jesus Christ.

Jimmy was late. He sauntered in at quarter past four, all sideways smirk and wriggle. Evie and Rose had exhausted all the gossip and polished off two brandy and ginger ales each. They turned to Jimmy, fluttering like petals in a breeze. 'What aboutcha, Jimmy?'

'Now girls, what'll it be?'

'I'll have another brandy,' said Evie, her tiny ringed hand blanketing his beefy paw. 'But *Rosie*, I'm afraid, has had enough.'

A squeal of protest curled from Rose's lips. A sound she never normally made.

His voice was a waltz, a glide. 'I hear Rose can *never* get enough. Right Rosie?' He dropped a silver-blue wink.

Rose flushed. '*You'll* never know!' Her pulse pounding in her neck. A ride in a car with no brakes.

Jimmy laughed and ambled toward the bar. The women were silent for several seconds.

'No harm in him,' said Evie finally. She patted her permed hair.

'Of course not. All talk.'

'All talk. Thinks the world of your Georgie.'

'Everyone thinks the world of Georgie,' said Rose.

The match wasn't being televised. Georgie flipped channels, looking for a score.

'You'll have another,' said Jimmy.

'I'm okay, thanks.'

'Your glass is empty.'

'I'm headed home to check the roast.'

'The what? You can't leave now. I just got here.'

'I'll be back.'

'Take a taxi so you can have a drink.'

'Sunday roast and all the trimmings. Interested?'

Jimmy laughed. 'What's got into you?'

Steaming vegetables in cool white bowls; the picture in his head helped Georgie breathe. Roast potatoes. Tender beef. He didn't know why. He just wanted it. Something basic, warm and good. He didn't know why.

'Nothin'. Tired of eating out of paper cartons. Aah, look at that.' The match had ended in a draw.

'Liverpool are useless these days.'

'I know.' His neck got tired looking up at Jimmy. 'So you'll eat with us?'

'I don't know, Georgie. Sounds like a waste of good drinking time to me.' Jimmy's voice had that musical sound, that roll, and he was combing the air with his fingers. He'd had a few before coming out. Georgie had that low-down crumbling-in-his-gut feeling.

Returning to our top story–

'Jesus, would you look at that?' Rodney pointed up at the television.

–over two hundred Spanish citizens have lost their lives–

'They look like toy trains,' said Rodney. 'Don't they? Like toys that got dropped. Or, no, run over. Don't they?'

'Turn it down,' Jimmy growled.

'Jesus.' A child, a little girl, on a stretcher. Torn.

Alison, Georgie thought.

'Do we not have enough of bombs in our own country? Change the fucking channel.' Jimmy sounded more tired than angry.

Georgie switched back to the horse racing.

'Makes you think, though. Doesn't it? That kind of thing. Really makes you think.' Rodney waited for one of the men to take him up on that, but neither did. Jimmy was shaking his head, staring at nothing. Georgie was checking his watch. Boring old farts, thought Rodney. Last time I try to raise the level of conversation. 'Right. Two brandies and a Guinness, was it Jimmy?'

'When Alison was small, we had proper cooked dinners. Especially on Sundays.' Georgie patted his ample belly.

Jimmy gave a ragged laugh. 'You did, yeah. And Rosie'd ring here every Sunday saying, "Tell him to put down his feckin' pint, his food is getting cold!"'

Evie thought her sister-in-law was beautiful. It wasn't how Rose looked but what she was. Jowly and square-shouldered in photos; in person she had a sleepy grace. She moved like water. Pale, with purpled lips and black hair and lively eyes that changed colour with the phases of the moon.

Sammy looked like Rose. But not enough. His colouring was haphazard, his extra flesh sagged. He was a nervy creature, always fidgeting. The first time she'd met Rose they were kids. Sammy was taking her to the pictures. Rose sat puffing a cigarette in the doorway. Evie'd known already she would marry Sammy. Just knew, in the way that girls do. And she'd looked at Rose, her languidness, her sharp eyes and long, white neck. And she'd seen in Rose her Sammy, rearranged into something more. Something near to perfect.

The drinks were hitting her now, turning the room soft-focus. She watched Rose cross the room to Georgie, kiss him quickly on the cheek as he shrugged on his coat. And she thought that in all the years since of being a wife to Sammy, loving Sammy, she had kept on watching Rose. Hungry for those flashes of perfection. She took out her hankie and quietly blew her nose.

'Will I leave you some money?' Georgie asked his wife.

Jimmy threw an arm around her waist and squeezed. 'You're joking! Am I not here to care for the fair Rose?' He smelled of ale. Rose lifted her chin and laughed. She let her weight rest on his arm, her face brush his shoulder. Her excitement a beam of light.

Georgie thought Jimmy was play-acting, that Romeo show. Sad old duffer. The girls playing along, making out like Jimmy's Elvis, teenager stuff. Didn't get it himself. Liked a good joke but liked people acting their age as well. Stuff it. He hated being the only one sober.

'Right, I'll love yous and leave yous.' Georgie shoved his hands in his pockets and ducked his head, preparing for wind and glare. Albert dropped his newspaper and scurried back to his post in time to open the door. As Georgie left, Albert looked carefully up and down the empty street.

'...boys' names, Georgie, Sammy. Jimmy. Boys, see? Our generation, born right after the war, we were...we thought we were something. Georgie, Sammy, Billy, Stevie, Bobby... factory jobs right out of school, married, the whole thing, baby coming, new car. Out in the pubs on the weekends, weekends became every night. Wives complaining, happy to take our pay packets off us. But fun? Fun was for young fellas and we were never that. Boys to men–' he snapped his fingers–'like that. Nothing in between.'

'So when'd she leave you then, Jimmy?' asked Rodney.

'Are you listening to me? I don't think you're taking in a word I'm saying. The factory, Son. The fucking Yankee-owned factory starts laying people off. No new investment. Belfast, a place they've seen on the news, a place where people blow the arse off each other. That's it. Old men with boys' names sitting in the pub. Finished. End of the fucking story.'

Rodney waited a respectful interval, then said quietly, 'Another pint there, Jimmy?'

'Nineteen seventy-nine.' Jimmy drained his glass and slid it across the bar. 'Twenty-five years ago. Took the kid with her.'

Rose felt like singing. It was all coming together. Brandy and Jimmy and the heat, the flush. A pulse in her fingers, a softening in her jaw. She sighed a glittering sigh and knew herself to be glorious. Waited for this all week.

'How's our Sammy?' she asked Evie.

'Ach, well, you know, Sammy is Sammy. I was talking to him this morning.'

'He's liking Saudi?'

'He loves it, he says the weather is just spectacular. Sunny and mild all the time. He's getting quite tan, he says.'

'Must be very hot.'

'Well, on the compound all the houses have air conditioning.'

'So you're looking forward to going?'

'Sure, why wouldn't I be? All that sunshine. And Sammy's taken to the work, so that's okay.'

Rose leaned forward until she could see her own reflection in Evie's glasses. 'And you're not at all nervous? I mean, on the news...'

Evie batted the thought away. 'Sammy says it's quite okay, when you're there you don't even think about it.'

Rose lit one of her firecracker smiles. 'We'll miss you around here.'

'Ach no, I mean...no. Will you? Really?'

Rose giggled and squeezed Evie's arm. Evie was blinded for a moment by the promise of the reach, the grasp, the warm pressure of her fingers and the fizz pop bang of her grin. Then Jimmy slid in next to Rose and made a show of grabbing her knee under the table. Rose screamed and slapped his arm, and everyone laughed, and it was like the moment had never happened. So many times afterward, Evie would wonder to herself if it really had.

Rodney brought the next round over on a tray. Rose poured her old drink in over her new one.

'I shouldn't, I shouldn't, I really shouldn't,' muttered Evie.

'You only live once,' said Rodney.

'Can't argue with that,' said Jimmy.

Rodney pulled a chair over and the four started chatting about nothing in particular. The club was nearly empty. From the telly came the monotonous roar of motor car racing.

'Where is everyone?' asked Rose.

'Home for their tea,' said Jimmy.

Rodney filled them in on the committee's plans to attract new members. Live music on Friday nights, snooker tournaments on Wednesdays. Karaoke twice a month. The three listened politely. Evie knew none of it would work. The dead can not be ressurected, not even with a karaoke machine. Too many old agonies in this room. Too much no one could talk about. Better to let it go.

Glorious, thought Rose, as she unbuttoned her top blouse button. Glorious, as Jimmy did his Ian Paisley imitation and they all fell about, cackling. The boy, Rodney, eyed her cleavage and Jimmy's thigh touched hers and THAT was glorious. The world was glorious. And she, she... was the world.

The meat was safe. The trifle was setting. Georgie fixed himself a cup of tea. Felt that he had captained a ship across dark waters. The dinner would be smashing.

Lately he'd thought they could be in trouble. Glazed and lazy with pills and potions, prescribed for vague complaints. Can't sleep, can't stay awake, can't take a shit. Soreness in the back. Sour crumbling in the gut. Pain. Dull but persistent.

Busyness, he felt, was key. Rose took little interest. In the garden, the cooking, anything he suggested. Smug by the fire with her crossword puzzle book. Proud of her expanding vocabulary. More words, less to say.

Georgie set the table.

And Liverpool had let him down. A draw with Middlesborough. Bollocks. Alison could make serviette swans. He settled for triangles.

A tinkling crash brought him to the window. The sinking sun threw shadows across the garden. He blinked, rubbed his eyes. Better go take a look.

The garden felt strange. Wind whipped the hanging laundry. The slanting light found texture on leaves, blades of grass, bricks and pots. Laburnum blazed and cherry blossoms danced. He stumbled slightly on the path.

The wind had knocked a statue down. One of the two plaster statues he'd picked up at the garden centre a few weeks ago. The Twins, he'd called them. Two ladies in togas with upswept hair, almond eyes, parted lips. Feeling oddly sensitive, he turned the remaining statue so it couldn't see the shards and dust that were once its sister. Then he gathered the dustpan and broom.

She found herself standing. Couldn't remember...the room came back to Rose like the headlights of an oncoming train. Rodney's voice, shapes of sound, no meaning. His Adam's apple bounced and the two angry spots on his chin quivered.

'Put on some music,' she mumbled.

'What was that, Gorgeous?' Jimmy asked from beside her.

'Nothing. I have to go to the toilet.'

He swung around sideways to let her pass. Just as her thighs were brushing his knees, he swung his arm in a lazy gesture and grabbed her left breast. Grabbed it hard, like he was drowning and she a life raft. Her breath came out through her teeth like a snake's. Jimmy snickered and let go. 'Catch yourself on,' Rose grunted and lurched away from the table. From far away she heard Evie calling, 'Rose? You okay?' Too much trouble to answer. She pushed through the door into the Ladies'.

Cool inside. Butterscotch and cream. Exhaust fan purring. She leaned on the cold edge of the sink, humming something, some old song she used to dance to.

Baby baby, baby baby...

She closed her eyes and swayed. Music. They should have music, a jukebox or something. There used to be music. She ran water in the sink and splashed some on her face. *Baby baby baby...*

She saw him first in the mirror. 'You're not supposed to be in here!' Didn't seem real. Still long and broad as the first time she'd seen him.

'I'm just checking on you, Gorgeous. Evie thought you didn't look well.' Jimmy lay a hand on the back of her neck. Soft. 'You look okay to me,' he said.

And then she was on him, against him, her tongue scraped his teeth. He lifted her on to the counter, it was wet, she wrapped her leg around his waist and held on. He breathed into her, gripped her by the hair. She thought he would eat her alive. Inside her eyelids were spirals of flame.

Then Jimmy leapt backwards as though she had pushed him. She didn't, she wouldn't. She stretched out her arms.

'Rosie, Rosie, Rosie...' He wouldn't look at her. 'C'mon. Let's go back out.'

'What? I thought you—Jimmy—'

'Hey now.' He took hold of her hand, kissed her knuckles. 'Don't know about you but I'm kinda drunk. Don't be angry, Rosie. You know you're my girl.'

Hot tears slid down her cheeks. Her lips opened and closed. 'I thought—Jimmy. I thought—'

He stepped towards her, red-faced. 'It was a bit of fun. No harm in it. I'm sorry, Rose. Sorry.'

He left her then. Stood in the hall by the cigarette machine, shaking and swaying and catching his breath. What a mess that could've been. For the cost of a quick fumble—shit! What got into her? How could he know? Not his fault. Not his bloody fault! The liquid heat of her—ohh. Forget it. Whiskey, a double. Forget it.

Nearly cost him—well, everything. Such as everything was. This place, Georgie, Sunday afternoons. That stupid bitch. Jesus. He pressed his forehead into the wall, closed his eyes. *Rosie.*

One small hand, that was how his thinking shifted. Her cheeks and lips, a sandaled foot, her shoulder he had swept away. Along with all the other bits he couldn't name. And the dust. But he couldn't bin the small white hand with its perfect tapered fingers. It lay in his palm and he stared at it, feeling strange and silly. Grown man hunkered on the back step looking at this bit of plaster. The sun sinking. Time passing. He ought to be getting on.

Alison. When she was small, her body had this same chiseled perfection. The wee fingers, the toes...the life inside her they had given her, he and God and Rose. How like Rose she was. Carbon copy. The same black-haired beauty. How proud he'd been with Rose on one side of him, Alison on the other. Holding both their white hands. Funny old Georgie, freckles and a squashed-up nose and his dumpy little body. But look what he had. Look what he'd been given. Hadn't he turned out well?

That child on the stretcher in Spain. She had a father. He'd be holding her hand right now. Georgie closed his fingers around the tiny plaster fingers and sighed. How easily things get broken.

Rose washed her face. The water was cold. It went in her mouth and up her nose. She choked and spat and kept on washing. Behind the wall pipes groaned.

The taxi was late. Georgie had closed the hall window, turned on a lamp in the front room, checked the back door. How many times had he done these things? How many times left to go? His father hadn't made it to the age he was now.

There was something else about that girl on the stretcher. It woke up something else, a memory that brushed against him late at night. Jeannie? Jenny? Vague, teasing memory. Her laugh.

The photo in the paper. She was carried out, covered by a white sheet. Battered beyond recognition, it said. Funny way to say it. He always heard it backward, as though they meant she'd been hit so many times she had stopped recognising this world, this life. And then she was gone.

In the mirror an acre of bloated flesh like sour milk, and her somewhere beneath. All the makeup in the world couldn't bring her to the surface. Her, the Rose she thought she knew. Where was Georgie? She had to go out there. Couldn't.

It all changed after that. He remembered seeing the club on TV, weathered and windowless, a blind old man. Crime tape across the door. One of the club's staff implicated, a young fella who'd worked the bar that night. He'd let them in. Escaped out the delivery entrance when they started on her.

All changed. Even after they'd been dealt with, the boys who did it. Boys! Knew them to see. Dealt with how, he didn't know. Well, yes, he did. But he was careful not to learn any details.

All changed. Like a spell was put on the place; people moved in slow motion, spoke in hushed tones. In the ten years since so many families had drifted away from the club.

How could you get your head around it? There were supposed to be limits. Rules. How could they do that to a girl, one of their own?

She was seeing some Catholic lad...that was the rumour. Turned out it wasn't even true.

Late at night, when the tablets weren't working, she would lie very still in the bed, trying not to wake Georgie. The darkness was an absence; the silence, the end of all sound. Time was not passing. She couldn't breathe. Who was she now? Not in motion, not at work. Not visible. Her baby grown and moved away, her home and husband humming along without her help. Cherry blossoms bloomed and dinner came to table without her lifting a finger. The space she occupied grew smaller and smaller. Hours and days could go by without anyone really seeing her. Who was she now?

Rose gathered up all the selves she had ever been and something else...something small and bright in her peripheral vision. Some Rose she had yet to be. And then she opened the door.

'Did you see yer woman on telly?'

'Which woman is this?'

'You know, the one from Belfast, what was on that train. The Spanish train that got blown up.'

Rodney was spinning the drinks tray on his finger. It caught the light and flashed like a metal moon, like cold fire. Evie closed her eyes but could still see sparks.

'That's awful. Terrible,' she muttered.

'Oh, she's not dead. She's in hospital, like, but she's not dead. They had her on telly. They was asking her what she saw and stuff. Dunno what part she's from. But Belfast anyway, they said Belfast.'

Jimmy sat across from Evie and she noticed his charm was turned down to a simmer. He was pretending to watch the motor car racing. To fill the silence, Evie asked, 'What was she doing in Madrid?'

'That's the funny bit.' Rodney leaned forward, arms on the table. 'They asked her that, they said, *and how did you come to be living in Spain?* And she's there in this ward with her head all bandaged and her leg in plaster, like, and she's all bruised and shit, and she says, *well, I had to leave Northern Ireland. I had to get away from all the violence!*'

Jimmy's snort of laughter ripped the air. Rodney ducked his head and smiled gratefully. 'She's there with all them swarthy fellas, watching the bull fights...'

'Pass the sangria!' giggled Jimmy.

'Pass the sangria, let's watch the bull fights and BOOM!' Rodney and Jimmy were in stitches.

Rose approached unnoticed. 'What's the joke?'

Jimmy struggled to his feet. 'Rose? Buy you a drink?'

'Do,' she said softly.

The taxi pulled up to the corner and Georgie scrambled out. Her laugh, her laugh...he remembered her laugh. He'd seen her, was it that night? Or some other? She was at the bar. Laughing loud. As if to convince somebody she was having a good time. Desperate sound.

Jeannie? Jenny? He rang the bell, remembering.

Rose was porcelain–pale, easily chipped. Evie made her sit while the men fetched the drinks. She thought, I've missed something. Something's happened and Rose won't say. Then she thought, I can't be bothered. I've had enough intrigue to last me a lifetime. I'll move away with Sammy soon and leave them to their dramas. Safe Sammy. Words cool and soft as raindrops on her skin. Safe Sammy, drip drop drip.

The bell rang.

Georgie came in from the cold and dark, into crowing, drumming, smoke-stale light. He blinked solidly in the doorway. Too long alone. Their voices too loud and he couldn't find his way out of his own head.

Yet they were glad to see him. Rose in full-sulk. Stroking his arm. She had missed him. Tilted head and downcast eyes, appealing to him, come and have a drink with me, he didn't know what to make of it. She was drunk, but something more, a whole layer of frosting missing. Three a.m. naked sort of drunk. And here it wasn't even seven o'clock.

Evie stood to one side. Curtains drawn, giving away nothing. God, he hated being the only one sober. He groped his way forward. Jimmy and the boy were head-to-head across the bar, sharing secrets. Rodney saw him and cleared his throat. Jimmy turned and his face, his big face was pink and flesh overwhelmed the bones. He was pink and polished as a glazed ham with marble-bright eyes and he said:

'You'll have another.'

As if Georgie had never left. As if their conversation had spooled out across the hours. Georgie wondered did he leave, was the garden and the statue and the cooking meat a dream?

And he said, 'Sure, go on.'

And it was a dream, pass the carrots and serviette swans. He was tired and the well-set table in East Belfast was a dream that fell to pieces when you woke. He couldn't imagine what he'd been thinking. He was so tired.

Sinking, they were sinking like the sun. He shrugged his way to the bar and there was a sudden machine gun spray of laughter from the telly. And Jesus, it was a desperate sound.

Albert consulted his clipboard one last time. Georgie Glass, his wife. A couple of their friends. A few other regulars, all left now, home for *Coronation Street*. That was how Sundays went. This lot was legless, they'd be here a while. That was okay. Might as well enjoy it while they could. He reckoned the numbers were so low, the club couldn't last much longer. Some day soon, they'd probably tear the whole place down.

KNOWING MY BROTHER

THIS CAN'T BE THE PLACE.

I'm in a ritzy apartment building on Nob Hill. I'm looking for my brother. A bald, lisping doorman presides over the foyer. In his spare time he could be a Truman Capote impersonator—the doorman, not my brother. He waves me toward the elevator, which carries me to Rob's floor. It is beige and mirrored, thick with the fat, slip-covered silence of the rich. I hesitate as the elevator doors thunk shut behind me. This just can't be right. How can he possibly afford this? Then the door opposite opens and out steps Rob. He is six feet, six inches tall without his boots, which he has spray-painted black. Gone is his unruly helmet of brown hair. The sides of his head were shaved clean moments ago, he explains, by his best friend and roommate Matt. The hair that is left has been pulled back into a quarter-inch ponytail and gelled into place. He sports a threadbare goatee that looks like it itches, and round midnight blue sunglasses. He catches sight of himself in the hall mirror and starts to laugh, a throaty sound that punctures the padded silence of the hall. It is the first thing about him that I recognise. He laughs harder and harder.

'Look at me,' he says. 'Something has gone horribly wrong.'

It is 1994. My brother is twenty-four and this is his first visit to the West Coast. He and Matt plan to spend their last summer before graduating college bartending and exploring San Francisco. What has paid Rob's airfare and the rent on this suite is a credit card some ill-advised bank has issued him. The card is up to its limit, as is Matt's, and as they have no jobs and no savings, they are wondering where dinner will come from. But there is a bottle of white wine in the fridge (it came with the suite) and they have an excellent view of the city, and cable TV too. They are not complaining.

They ask me eagerly which neighbourhoods they should check out first. I smile a competent older-sister smile and pull out my street map.

I haven't seen Rob in...three years? Four? Since we last met he has become a Philosophy major with a bartender's licence, a prescription for Prozac and a habit of disappearing for weeks at a time. Our mother refers to him as, "(sigh) Robert" or, sometimes, "The Prodigal Son". My own habits have not been deemed colourful enough to warrant a nickname, nor laboured sighs. My brother inherited most of the colour. I inherited the map-carrying gene.

In my adult life I have had many close male friends and have fondly said of each of them, 'He is like a brother to me.' Thirty minutes in the company of my actual brother disproves this assertion. Or rather it proves my brother is not like a brother to me. I love him but don't understand him. The things that are familiar about him—his smile, his fondness for repeating Monty Python routines, his sputtery firecracker anecdotes—are familiar because they remind me of me. As I watch him, watching the lights of the city like a prince from his tower on the hill, I think that I don't really know who he is. And I'd like to.

So I ask him if he'd like to have dinner some night next week. Just us, my treat. 'Ho! Sounds great.'

When is he free?

'At the moment, I'm free pretty much all the time.'

'Free as birds,' Matt echoes, laughing.

Rob flops down on his bed and stares up at the blinking Christmas tree lights he and Matt have ringed around the suite. Blink. Blink. 'Nothing in the date book. No plans.'

A few days later Rob calls me to say he can't make dinner on the evening we had scheduled. He will be taking inventory in a lamp store that night. He and Matt have had no luck finding bartending jobs. The field is closed to those with no connections and no union card. So they have registered with a temp agency, and because they are both in the "no special skills" category, they get jobs like the one at the lamp store, where they work alongside chattering grandmothers and men with 1970s haircuts and socks that don't match. In fact, for the lamp store gig, Rob is asked to be in charge of the temps, which he guesses is sort of like being chosen head lunatic, flattering if you don't think about it too hard. Being in charge means walking around with a clipboard, and he notices that every time he picks up the clipboard the other lunatics besiege him with questions...about *lamps*. It is as though they don't recognise him as one of their own, a temp who knows nothing about lamps and doesn't need to know anything except how to count them. With the clipboard in his hands he becomes an *authority*. He wonders if he has stumbled onto a life lesson here. Perhaps one does not need courage or wisdom to be respected as a leader. Perhaps all one needs is a clipboard.

When my brother was a teenager he had a poster of Martin Luther King Jr. on his wall. It was to the right of a poster of Cheryl Ladd, of 'Charlie's Angels' fame, kneeling on a bed in a satiny-blue slip. On Martin Luther King Day Rob taped a smaller picture of the leader to one of our living room windows so it could be seen from the street. This was when we lived in South Philadelphia. That evening we found, scrawled in white chalk on the brick front of our house, the message *Robert is a nigger lover!*

Robert put his hands on his hips, threw out his scrawny fourteen-year-old chest and laughed. 'Better than being white trash,' he said in a voice so fierce mom shushed him, although it was dinner time and there was no one else out on the street to hear.

The calls started before he even arrived in San Francisco. My mother and stepmother both called, wanting to know when he would arrive, where he would be staying, what would he do for work, didn't he have anything lined up? Well, what were his plans? I was useless to them. 'He'll get here when he gets here,' I said. I could feel their frustration. I heard my mother suck sharply on her cigarette; heard Cathy, my stepmother, pause and place the casserole dish she had been washing into the drying rack with a clatter.

'But he must have told you—'

'No, he didn't say. Maybe you should ask *him*.'

But when they tried, they discovered his number at school had already been disconnected. School was out; no one at the college knew where he was. He had not been in touch with anyone for five weeks.

When I was a kid it was my job to look out for my brother. I had the irrational feeling, when the phone calls came, that I was falling down on the job.

Once he arrived, their refrain became:

'Well, you've seen him, so—'

'How does he seem?'

'Does he still have that funny haircut?'

Actually, he doesn't. It is June and he now has a different funny haircut. The goatee and the ponytail are gone. The flat-top Mohawk, or something, remains. I like it, I've decided. The hair in combination with his height says, 'Not only that, but—'

When he was a teenager Rob hated being noticed. We'd be sitting on a bus and he would decide that everyone was looking at him. He would fidget, comb his hair with his fingers, slide down in his seat. 'What the hell is their problem?' he would hiss. I never saw who he was talking about, but to contradict him made him worse. So I looked straight ahead, my skin scalded by his anger and by the invisible, staring eyes.

He doesn't do that now. I laugh all the time when I am with him. He and his friend Matt have a slang all their own. They drop the word 'schmedley' into sentences in place of any noun. As in, 'pick me up a pack of schmedleys' or 'we almost froze our schmedleys off.' My favourite schmedley was when my brother said to me in dead earnest, 'Well now, that's a horse of a different schmedley!'

We go out to dinner at the Stinking Rose and giggle at the singing and dancing garlic bulbs painted on the walls. After dinner we drink at Vesuvio's and talk about our love lives. He describes the girl he wishes he were dating but isn't. And the girl he couldn't break up with because she didn't speak enough English to understand him. I describe the guy I thought I was dating who isn't returning my calls. I try to sound brave about this.

A week later I decide to confront the guy and I go to the restaurant where he works as a waiter. I arrange to have my brother, my roommate and another girl friend arrive at the restaurant about ten minutes after I do. This way I will not have to flee, alone and embarrassed, and will also not have to eat alone. We all meet at my apartment beforehand. I am pacing and changing my outfit until the last second. My women-friends do what women friends do and my brother rises to the occasion beautifully, promising to inflict bodily harm on the boy if he breaks my heart. My brother would never hurt anyone, but I appreciate him saying it.

In the end I do get my heart broken. My supporters arrive on cue and buy me drinks and cheer me up. We get spectacularly drunk and my brother and I act out scenes from *Life of Brian* at the table. When the waiter who broke my heart says to my brother, 'I've heard a lot about you,' he replies, 'I've heard a lot about *you*,' in a voice that makes the waiter stammer. It is the most fun I have ever had getting dumped.

I don't remember what year it was that Robert was institutionalized for the weekend. I remember it as happening in winter. But I may be remembering a different time, when Rob was joining a fraternity and got drunk with some of his new friends, ending up with a concussion.

The way he got the concussion was that he was stumbling through the woods alone at night and slipped on a patch of ice. That is how I know that happened in winter. I imagine I remember what it looked like, Robert lying in the perfect, star-kissed darkness among pine needles and the bony roots of ancient trees, dazed and alone. But then I remember I wasn't there. I was living in Massachusetts and he was in school in New Hampshire. I wasn't there to witness. So many important family events happen off-camera for me. I weigh the varying reports that come in by phone and letter, and I reconstruct the way it must have been. So I see him, alone for an immeasurable length of time, noticing the fog of his breath in the moonlight and not knowing what had happened, or what would happen, feeling separate from the before and after, the cold and everyone. Lost, in the purest sense. Maybe that is why I put the concussion and the institution together in my mind. I can't picture the inside of a mental institution. But I can see the woods on a winter night. So every time I think of the institution weekend, I picture my brother shivering in the woods at night, lost to everyone, to us, to himself. And that is the picture that makes the most sense.

He was locked up for the weekend—it might have been three days, I'm not sure—because his school counsellor thought he was a danger to himself. He was having vivid dreams about suicide. He was putting out cigarettes on his arms and hands. I guess he was drinking a lot. My brother denies he was a danger to himself. He was furious with the counsellor, who, he says, tricked him into going up to this place to begin with. He claims he didn't know the papers he signed were voluntary commitment papers, and the first moment he realised this was not some kind of ski trip, he tried to split. The reason he was there so long is simply that the doctor who had the power to evaluate and release people was away for the weekend. That is how I know it happened over a weekend.

It was my step-mom who first told me the institution story. Large parts of it made no sense to either of us. I have since talked to my brother about it, but he won't help me understand it. I don't know if he is telling me the complete truth about it. I think he is, but I don't know. Robert and I are self-invented people. We both have the feeling we are making it up as we go along. Rob once phoned Cathy to tell her he believes he is a lesbian trapped in a man's body.

So who knows which parts are true? The concussion was true because there were doctor bills to prove it. And the basic institution story is true because the counsellor phoned my step-mom. Beyond that, I don't know. I don't begrudge my brother his fictitious misadventures. I envy his nerve. But I can't tell the person from the myth.

Rob disappeared for three weeks after the night I was dumped by the waiter. No one answered his phone. This, as it turned out, was because he moved. He and Matt moved into a studio apartment with four other people.

They couldn't even pretend to afford Nob Hill anymore. Rob's bedroom is the kitchen doorway, his blanket the Irish flag that used to hang on his dorm room wall.

One July night at midnight, Rob and Matt come by the café where I work. They have just left the club across the street. They are dispirited. They went to the club because the girl of Matt's dreams works there. But tonight is her night off. So they drink Budweiser with rednecks for no purpose. And they have to be at work tomorrow morning. The temp agency has placed them at a bank where they tell me their main function is to amuse their supervisor with tales of their exploits while *she* works. Every so often they are called upon to lick envelopes or Xerox something. But mostly they recount and regale. It's a sweet deal, they say, except Rob feels ill every time he is in the bank—something with the fluorescent lighting or the re-circulated air. Anyway. Matt wants to head home but Rob persuades him to stop in an Irish pub down the street for a pint of Guinness to kill the lingering taste of Bud. I need to close the café and set up for the morning. So I suggest I might meet up with them there later. They can regale me with tales of their exploits. Okay, Rob says.

When I get to the pub, they have gone.

POTENTIAL

THE STREET WAS EMPTY and Tom was glad. No eyes. He could walk to the end of the block and not wonder what he looked like doing it. He could smile, skip, whatever he felt like. If only he knew what he felt like.

He noticed the brass nameplates on polished white stone. He slid his hands into his pockets and whistled into the great silence—his impression of a normal, happy guy. So he was sticking with happiness? Yes, he was. He'd been a happy guy for twenty-four years. Not constantly; he wasn't gaga. But generally, over all. Happy. And if there was something wrong with that, they'd have to explain it to him.

'Come in.' The room was not where he expected. Not down the long hall just off the waiting area, but behind a door he had thought was a coat closet. It wasn't much bigger than a closet and it had no window. He had to slide past her to get inside. Once inside there was nowhere to go but to the sagging couch against the far wall. He folded himself onto the couch, feeling sweaty and gigantic.

'Any trouble finding us?' She sat down on an orange plastic chair just inside the door and crossed her legs. Over jeans and a regular sweater she wore a white lab coat.

'No, no problem. Behind the hospital, a block from Golden Gate Park. Simple.'

'Yes, Professor Abrams said you'd been to the hospital recently. A head injury?' With her pen she tapped the file folder that lay across her lap. Reminding him he was a patient. What else had Abrams said?

'Just the ER for a couple hours. No big deal. I got knocked on the head, my boss didn't want to take a chance. No concussion or anything. Just an ordinary bump on the head.' I am ordinary. 'Professor Abrams didn't think it was related, did he?' Related to what? They would have to tell him. None of this was his idea.

She jiggled her pen thoughtfully. 'It could be a factor. How did it make you feel?'

He squeaked. In his head it was a snicker, but out loud it was a squeak. Her pen stopped jiggling.

'Why is that funny?'

Oh God, not again. 'It isn't, it's just kind of therapy-speak. *How did that make you feel?* You know?' He wished he could go out and come back in, start over.

But she smiled, slightly. 'Oh, okay. I see what you mean.' She wasn't bad. Young, not much older than him and very small, slim. No boobs at all. That was disappointing. Boobs would've made her...more sympathetic. But what the hell.

'What I was getting at was, did the blow to the head affect you emotionally? Can you remember how you felt just after?'

Sick. Legs shaking, buzzing in his ears. Lost in colours whenever someone spoke. Everything an effort. Tears rising to his eyes when he heard Molly's voice on the phone. 'Nah, can't really remember.' He sat back, crossed his legs in what he hoped was a casual, manly fashion. 'Just a headache.'

'Hmm. How did it happen?'

'Slipped on a wet floor. Bounced my head off a stainless steel counter.'

'Ow! Sounds awful.'

He enjoyed her sympathy, enjoyed the way her mouth puckered when she said "ow". 'My own fault.' He shrugged. 'We were short-staffed, busy. I was running.'

'You're a waiter?'

'Night manager. I got promoted a couple months ago. It's just a small bistro, but with...potential.'

'And what about you?'

'What about me what?'

'What about your potential?'

So here it was. She was getting down to business. Having lulled him with compassion for his poor cracked head.

He would happily have gone on talking about work, the customers who knew his name. The cool, perspiring neck of a wine bottle fragile in his hand. The stolen seconds of late night back-door cigarette breaks with the dishwasher. The steam on the windows soft-focussing the outside world. He would've liked to tell her about that.

But potential. She was definitely zeroing in.

Stiff-haired Mrs Winters with the voice like weak tea. 'Thomas is a very capable boy. But I'm afraid he isn't working up to his potential.' His mother's disappointed gaze that left him struggling for air. And afterward, her holding his hand—too tightly, always too tightly—as they walked home, his little sister Iris trailing behind as always. Iris, to whom everything was given and of whom nothing was expected; she trudged around all the time like an exiled queen, her pout indicating she was meant for better things. He thought that someone should deal with Iris. But they never got around to it because they never finished dealing with him.

'It's that job,' said his mother. Her words were hard, bits of gravel in the wind. 'I knew it was a mistake. You're too young to balance school and work.'

'I'm fourteen!' Then, in the sculpted tone he was learning to use on her: 'Anyway. We need the money.'

'We'd find another way,' she insisted. But the creeping doubt in her voice told him he would win. He smiled to himself and patted the bulge his new wallet made in his nylon windbreaker.

It was a warm spring evening. Porch lights bloomed. Tomorrow was Saturday, a work day. He'd finished the inventory and Mr Healey had promised he could wait on customers.

But now there was Mother's Mood. He read it in the pressure of her dry, fleshy hand, in the weariness of her walk and in the silence between them (underscored by the singing of lawn sprinklers and the snuffling of Iris, who suffered from hay fever). The Mood was his to fix. Once his father would've done it, with winks and whispers and kisses in the hollow of her throat. She'd push him away, giggling. The giggle had died with Dad. Now it was up to Tom, who had fewer tools at his disposal. 'Let's go to Ernie's,' he blurted.

The walking stopped. 'We don't need anything,' said his mother uncertainly.

'Let's get cold cuts for dinner.'

'I was going to make that casserole—'

'It's late; you don't want to start cooking now. We'll get ham and Swiss cheese. And those crusty rolls you like.'

'And what about vegetables, young man?' Her lips considering a smile.

'Coleslaw. Lettuce and tomato on the sandwiches. Come on.'

'Cream soda.' Iris had caught up with them. She was sucking on a strand of her hair, disgusting.

'Cream soda,' he promised her, 'and those big fat pickles from the barrel. And éclairs from the bakery for dessert.'

'Eww. I want ice cream.'

'An ice cream cone for you. Cherry vanilla.'

The despised Iris sighed in contentment. '*Please* mom,' she said, tugging on Mother's free arm. 'Pretty please with sugar on top?'

'And how are we going to pay for all that?'

'I've got it covered!' It was the line he'd been longing to say. The smile he was longing to smile because it always made her smile back. At her young man, who had so much potential that he could afford to squander a little. She smiled and the world grew softer. He thought he would always have it covered.

'If there was anything I could do—' Professor Abrams' pudgy hands were splayed across his desk in a helpless gesture.

'I know,' said Tom.

'Your work shows potential...great potential.'

'Yes Sir. Thank you.'

'But we can't base grades on potential.'

'No.'

'Grades are based on output.'

'Sure. Yes Sir.'

'And your output, let's face it—'

'I know—'

'It's crap is what it is.'

'Yes Sir.'

'We can't award scholarships for crap.'

'No Sir.'

'I'm sorry Son.'

'I know Sir. I appreciate it. I really do.'

'Do you?' Abrams got to his feet. He stepped out from behind his desk.

'I do,' said Tom. 'Really, you've done a lot for me already, don't think I don't realise that. The scholarship for this year...well, it made all the difference. Without it I couldn't have come back to school at all.'

'And now it's gone. How will you pay for your final year?' Abrams began to pace.

'I don't know. I guess I'll have to, you know, cross that bridge when I come to it.'

'You *have* come to it.' The pacing quickened. 'You're at the bridge, you're at the bridge now. How do you cross it? What will you do? You're twenty-four. You can't string this out forever.'

Tom flinched. Light stabbed at his eyes. He retreated to a cool, shadowy room inside himself. When he opened his eyes Abrams was still pacing. Tom pushed out of his chair and hurried to the door.

'Where are you going?'

His hand on the cold brass doorknob. 'Well, you've given me a lot to think about, Sir. I appreciate it and I'll let you know—I know your time is valuable, so—'

'For heaven sake, sit down Son. We need to sort this out.'

'Well, the fact is Sir, I'm running late. I need to get to work.'

Abrams nodded. His lips were pink and wet and too big for his face. His cardigan was missing a button. Where the button should have been two pieces of thread waggled limply. It was enough to make you want to cry somehow. 'That little bistro on Foster. That's where you work, isn't it?'

'Well, yeah...'

'Fine.' In a sudden jaunty movement, he retrieved his umbrella from the stand by the door. 'I'll walk with you.'

Abrams' red umbrella opened against the grey sky. He stared at it in surprise. 'Where in blazes did this come from? Must be my wife's. She's partial to red.' He looked at Tom, still cowering in the doorway. 'Haven't you got an umbrella?'

'I must have left it—' Where? Somewhere in the maze of his day.

'Well, come on. Get under. No point getting soaked.'

Huddled in the umbrella's blush, they descended the stone steps to the sidewalk. Tom stared at Abrams' hand clutching the curved handle. Pale and pudgy, with age spots like spilled coffee. Nails impossibly thick and yellowed. Not a hand, a strange, soft undersea creature.

Abrams sniffed. 'Smell that? Rosemary. Grows wild on the hill there. Rosemary, for remembrance. So the poets say.' They reached the sidewalk, turned left. 'You remember him at all? Your father?'

Tom was annoyed. The old man was pushing it, pretending they shared intimacy instead of mere proximity. 'Yeah. Of course.'

'How old were you when he died?'

'Eight.'

Abrams shook his head. 'Hell of an age. Not that there's a good age to lose your dad. I was eleven when mine went.'

'Oh.' For the life of him, Tom couldn't imagine Abrams age eleven. 'I'm sorry. What happened?'

'Cancer. Yours?'

'Car accident. Wet roads.' Tom nodded at the silvery rain. 'He always drove too fast.'

'In a hurry. Like you.'

'I guess.'

A funny, fond look took over Abrams' face. If he hugs me, Tom thought, I'm out of here.

Instead he said, 'What are your goals, Son? Where do you see yourself in ten years' time?'

'Foster Street's this way.' He guided them left again, cutting through Caulfield Hall's parking lot.

'Tom? Did you hear me?'

'Yes Sir.'

'Well? Do you like school?'

Tom started to laugh, a gasping, hiccupy laugh.

Abrams looked alarmed. 'What is it, are you alright? What's so funny?'

'I don't know,' said Tom, and he didn't. With an effort he stopped laughing. 'I never thought of it. I never thought whether I liked it or not. It's just what you do.'

'Maybe you should talk to someone.'

'Why?'

'You seem a little confused.'

'I'm fine Sir, honestly. I'm happy. Not about losing the scholarship, of course. But generally. You don't need to worry.'

'Maybe you should talk to someone about your future.'

'I never saw much point in that.'

'That's just what worries me. Son, what do you want for yourself? What do you want to be?'

'A success,' said Tom. And he strode into work, where the customers greeted him by name.

STUPID SLIM-NECK
AUDREY HEPBURN DREAMS

THE NEW LOIS EATS only carrot sticks and yogurt. ONLY. And only non-fat coffee-flavoured yogurt. Because strawberry is for children and Lois is not a child. Lois is nearly fifteen. The new Lois eats her yogurt in baby-sized slurps off the tip of the spoon because it lasts longer that way. For example, one container of yogurt sees Lois through to the second commercial break of *General Hospital*, which usually occurs at 3:14. Sometimes 3:17.

The new Lois patiently peels carrots every morning, while her parents rush around getting ready for work. She likes being a quiet thing, like the couch or a picture on the wall. She likes to focus on the carrots, on their colour, that blood-hot orange colour against her pale hands. She likes to focus on that and not on her parents and their fighting. ('We're not fighting, we're talking,' says her mother.)

Just by thinking of carrots she reduces her parents' voices to the buzzing of distant bees.

Sometimes the carrot sticks stay nice in the fridge. But sometimes by late afternoon they are withered and stooped, like little old men. New Lois eats them anyway. She forces her mind around a corner, beyond the rubberiness of the carrots. She thinks about something else. For example, *General Hospital*.

The new Lois walks. Walking is good exercise. It's summer, though, and there's nowhere to walk to. The city has that empty, used-up feeling. And it's hot. Lois won't wear shorts because her legs are round and white like bowling pins. Also when she walks her inner thighs rub together and it hurts like a burn. Her bra straps dig into her shoulders and every part of her jiggles and wobbles. But she walks.

Lois has always wanted to be on TV. Sometimes she sits on the bus and practices tipping her head and smiling a wholesome smile. She imagines the safety of being boxed-in on that small screen. Being looked at without having to look back, except at the camera with a sort of generalized warmth that would make people feel reassured. She waits to be discovered.

The new Lois was born when Lois *was* on TV, the one and only time. She was in the audience for the local morning chat show, *AM Philadelphia*. She went because they were doing a behind-the-scenes look at *General Hospital*. But it turned out that part was pre-recorded in California. The audience watched it on a monitor. It was no different from watching it at home. Still, they showed some of her favourite actors learning their lines, having their hair done and talking about how much they owed their fans. Then reaction shots were taped in the studio. The audience was told to clap and smile, clap and smile! Bigger, bigger! Lois smiled the biggest she could and even managed a small wave. She felt, in that moment, like Audrey Hepburn.

Her best friend Pammy taped the show and they watched it together that evening. Just at the end, the camera found Lois.

Stupid slim-neck Audrey Hepburn dreams bit the dust. That thing, that squinting, thick-fingered thing, that mountain in a sweatshirt and stretch pants...as the thing waved at the camera, new Lois flamed to life.

New Lois walks to the pharmacy on 23rd because it is air-conditioned. She stands and reads the movie magazines and feels the sweat slide cold down her back. No one in the place cares if you read the magazines. There is usually just one girl behind the counter and she is usually reading a magazine too. Lois does not look at the candy display. She does not look at the Reese's Peanut Butter Cups in their friendly orange wrappers. She holds out as long as she can and then plunges back into the raw, honest heat that burns the call of chocolate and peanut butter out of her head.

An air conditioner drips. It's 1:48. An hour and twelve minutes until *General Hospital*.

Lois is so hungry she almost can't stand it. Her stomach bubbles and gurgles like a fish tank. She pictures it that way, glass-encased, with angry orange fish swimming in circles. She hates her stomach. She'd cut it out if she could. Slice away her ass cheeks and mottled thighs. Peel away her calves. Leave bone and joint, hard and curved and graceful.

She passes the Lombard Swim Club. The sidewalk at the entrance is wet. Smell of chlorine, damp cement and suntan lotion; distant shrieks and splashes. She and Pammy used to come here. When they were small and their bodies went straight up-and-down. Then Pammy's family got a summer house at the shore—*a bungalow*, her mother called it—no room for guests. Pammy's mother wears lots of face powder and her glasses are on a little chain. She sits on a lot of committees. She seems really busy, which is funny because Lois' mother says that Pammy's mother is a perfect example of the idle rich. But she doesn't seem idle. Neither does Lois' mom; the main difference is at the end of the day, her own mom looks sweaty and sighs a lot and her hair sticks to her face. Pammy's mom never looks sweaty. Lois wonders which kind of busy she will be when she grows up. Sticky-sweaty and angry-busy, or powdered-polished and marble-cold, glasses-on-a-chain-busy? She can't imagine inhabiting either possibility. She doesn't think it's up to her, anyway.

She misses Pammy. Misses the oblivion of swimming underwater. Headless legs and torsos, sightless and indifferent. Misses the days of straight up-and-down.

Broken glass glitters in the sun. Green. Lois finds it beautiful.

A gang of kids stand by the corner shop, eating ice cream cones. New Lois looks away. She isn't, is not, a kid.

Home. She avoids herself in the elevator mirror; gratefully dives into the apartment's shaded silence. 2:51. Pushes the button and the television welcomes her, blossoming bright and loud.

The new Lois heads to the fridge. Lifts out one non-fat coffee yogurt and one Tupperware container of carrot sticks. So hungry she is shaking.

Then, on the counter, a box of donuts. Country-glazed. With a note from her mother. 'Lois, for God sake. Eat!'

General Hospital's theme music plays. Lois starts to sob.

EVE

'THERE IT GOES AGAIN.' The white limousine snaked down the hill. At the bottom it turned toward the towers of downtown and disappeared, taillights absorbed last by the darkness. Tom rubbed fog from the window with his hand. 'That's the sixth time he's circled the block.'

'You exaggerate,' said Molly.

'No I don't. Well yeah, I do, sometimes, but I'm not now. Six times!' He slapped the table for emphasis.

Molly frowned with half her mouth. 'I hate it when you get drunk before me.'

The door opened again. Smell of wet pavement and Chinese food from Wing Tun's down the street. Sound of the rain's galloping hooves. Screechy giggling as two women struggled to close their umbrellas in the doorway. They leaned against each other, all damp hair and laughter, and Molly was suddenly so lonely she thought she might cry.

'Where's the waitress? Jesus.' She looked around without seeing anything. The door thumped shut.

Tom liked the way the cool damp window felt on his forehead. His eyes liked the green and violet stripes, neon reflected on the rain-slick surface of the street. Life hummed. Life was good. White steam kissed the window when he spoke. 'They're really busy. Might have to order at the bar.'

'Jesus.'

'I'll go, I'll go. Whadda ya want? I'll go.' Coins jingled reassuringly in his pockets as he lurched to his feet. 'Another beer?'

'Make it a brandy.'

'Righto,' he said. He would make it okay. Good intentions filled his sails like a clean breeze and he was off.

Molly pushed away her empty glass with its gaping mouth and checked her watch again. Just eleven. One more time around the circle and then Auld Lang Syne and squeaky blowers and damp kisses and confetti. Another hour to get through before the vast crowd started counting together. Then a few minutes of strangers hugging and everyone laughing and she's in on the joke...for a few minutes.

Tom stumbled down the tightly-curled stairs to the men's room. Bright fluorescence. He blinked. There was a condom machine on the wall offering condoms of different flavours. Wild Strawberry, Piña Colada, Licorice Whip.

What a world! His laughter echoed in the throbbing whiteness. God, he loved this city. Anything was possible here. Long white limos and licorice dicks! Fantastic!

He caught a glimpse of himself in the mirror, laughing. Crazy. His face looked like a rubber mask. Carefully he brought it under control, feature by feature. With elaborate sobriety he asked his reflection for a brandy and another margarita. There. Still a geek, but presentable.

A fresh start, that was all they needed. And wasn't that what this night was all about?

'Any resolutions?'

His name was Steven and he was sharing their table. That was all. How could she have said no? The place was packed and here in this narrow window booth there was space for, well, at least two more. This was what she would say to Tom when he complained. Which he wouldn't, not in front of Steven. He'd come back to the table with the drinks and he'd raise his eyebrows quizzically at her and his face would go all puppyish with disappointment. He liked them to be an island. She did too, or she had...she wasn't sure which it was. She liked the snug feeling when it was just the two of them. But then sometimes they were two islands with only a rickety bridge between them...God, her head was full of drivel tonight. With relief she focused on Steven.

He had said there was a "someone" who "might be" meeting him here later. Molly hadn't asked if the someone was female. She thought probably yes. Steven had a settled air about him. Though no ring. She gestured to let him know she couldn't hear him and he leaned forward across the table. He aimed his voice to her ear and his breath was warm. He smelled of whiskey, lemon and rainwater. She told herself to quit smelling him.

'Any resolutions?' he said again.

'Oh! Not really. I mean, I haven't exactly thought about it.' Okay, she was now officially the most boring person on the planet. Try again. 'Except—well, I do plan on reading more. Classics, I mean. I just think it's important to be well-read. Don't you?' She had no idea where that came from, but never mind—he was nodding. He looked like a reader, which she now realised was why she had said it in the first place. She was trying. Oh God, she was trying! She felt a flush rise from the base of her neck. She wished Tom would hurry up and come back; she wished Tom would stay away for hours.

The rain had stopped.

It was the stillness that drew him, the sudden breathless silence; the razor-sharp stars visible in the slice of sky above the alley. Tom stepped outside. The delivery doors were propped open by empty kegs. Two barmen slouched nearby, shirt-tails out, sucking on cigarettes frantically. The air was fresh and salty. At the entrance to Columbus Avenue stood an old Chinese man, wrapped in a windbreaker several sizes too large, holding a white bucket full of single, cellophaned roses. 'Flower for your girlfriend?' he called to Tom.

'Okay. How much?' Tom moved forward on unsteady legs. He was thinking simultaneously of Molly's face when he presented her with the rose and of the bank machine across the street, which he should probably visit again.

'For you? Three-fifty.' The old man whistled as he made change. Tom muttered a thanks and took a red rose from the bucket. The old man winked. 'Wise choice. She a lucky woman.' Tom laughed and the old man limped away down Columbus Avenue.

The avenue was flirting. The white marquee of the Erotic Cabaret dazzled like a smile; taxis splashing through puddles sounded like sighs. The fast-food place on the corner blushed heartbeat red and the sign above the Glass Onion glittered and winked. Café Roma's doors scraped open and the smell of espresso drifted thickly down the pavements like syrup. Everything dripped and gleamed as though freshly painted, and the moon itself couldn't outshine the diamond-glow of headlights as cars rocketed off Broadway and down the steep hill.

Tom held the curving street in his hands like a picture postcard. It was his. It was splendid.

For weeks she'd seen the world in grainy black and white; people spoke and their voices came to her from across great distances. Inside her head was a buzz, a growl, a bad plumbing sort of sound that never went away. Ever since the move...it started with not recognising street names and ended with her not recognising herself. When had she gotten so fragile and fuddled? So hesitant, all the time blinking up at bus stop signs and gazing shyly into store windows. All the time searching for something. This she had tried to tell Tom because it seemed really important. All their time together they had spent searching; this move into the city was more of that, of looking for something. And what kept her awake at night was the feeling that she'd forgotten what they were looking for. She was afraid the search had no object anymore; searchers were all they were.

Tom didn't understand. Tom was happy. Tom had a gift for happiness, which was the first thing she'd loved about him. Trying to explain a worry to Tom was like trying to explain shadows to the sun. Better to bask in that heat while it lasted and contemplate shadows later, alone.

'I'd have to say *Nausea*.'

Jesus. She'd completely lost track of the conversation. 'Sorry. What?'

'I know it's not the most uplifting, but its influence can't be ignored.'

'Umm...no.'

Steven tugged at his beard and smiled. '*Nausea*. Jean-Paul Sartre? One of the most important novels of the twentieth century, in my opinion.'

Jesus, he *was* a reader! Either that or he memorised this stuff to impress girls in bars. And that would just be too sad. 'Oh, Sartre! Okay. He was a whaddayacallit—'

'An Existentialist!' cried Steven, looking way too excited. 'There's a quote from Celine at the start of the book—"He is a fellow without any collective significance, barely an individual." That's from *The Church*. What he's getting at is—'

...And he's off, thought Molly, watching Steven's lips move. She did her best to look fascinated, while each word he spoke sank to the green depths of her mind, sending not one bubble of meaning to the surface.

It was so frustrating. The person she wanted to get to know was not Steven, but herself. Steven was supposed to provide clues, reflect back to her this person she was becoming. New Molly, who lived in San Francisco. Who slept with the bathroom light on. Who would spend the last hour of the year talking to a stranger in a bar. (Where the hell was Tom, anyway?)

But of course, she told herself, women are the mirrors. Women reflect back to men a flattering image of themselves; that's mostly what flirting is, if you're a woman. She'd forgotten.

Tom would hate this guy. The thought made her grin, which she hid in an appraising 'Hm-m-m' as Steven made a point about Camus. Oh God yes. Tom would be kicking her under the table, humming 'Idiot Wind'. He had a Bob Dylan song for every occasion, it was part of their secret language. 'Idiot Wind' followed by 'Knocking on Heaven's Door': what an asshole, let's go home.

Steven laughed. 'Here we are, it's New Year's Eve and raining like crazy and we're here in this crowd discussing Existentialism. How perfect is that?'

And then she saw him. His blonde hair bleached white by the streetlights, his thin shoulders bowed under an invisible weight. Shrunken. A cold hand squeezed her heart, she tried to get up, forgetting she was folded into the narrow window booth. Tom was standing at the kerb, too small and hunched, figures pushing past him, there was something wrong...he wasn't like himself. He was looking down, which he never did, and twisting in his hands was something long and thin and bloodied at the top. She blinked and the dripping knife of her imagination turned into a flower.

Molly was too disturbed to wonder why Tom was outside in the first place. Pressure was building behind her eyes, she touched her fingers to the damp pane of glass as if he could feel this, so far away from her...Remembering Steven, she opened her mouth to say a hundred things and only managed, 'It's not raining anymore.'

The street had filled like a theatre lobby at intermission. In line to use the bank machine, Tom had closed his eyes and let gauzy bits of conversation reach him. '...strangest infection I ever had.' 'I'd go out with him tomorrow if he'd just change his name.' He had smiled, thinking how lucky he was to have Molly waiting for him. He clutched the rose tighter.

He hadn't done enough up till now; he knew that. He hadn't yet made of himself the man that she deserved. But here it would be different. Here, he could be anyone.

His wallet again fat, he elbowed his way to the kerb. The white limo sped by him, a shark slicing through black water. He craned his neck to watch it as people pushed past him into the intersection.

'Real monstrosity, huh?' It was an older man, silver hair and a bit of a belly. He was dressed stylishly in black trousers and a white dress shirt, the armpits of which were dark with sweat. He nodded in the direction of the vanishing limousine.

Tom shook his head at him. 'It's gorgeous,' he said. 'It *glides*.'

The man laughed loudly. 'Okay buddy, whatever you say.'

Tom knew he was laughing at him because his voice sounded drunk. 'I've maybe had a few drinks,' he explained to the man, 'but it's New Year's Eve. So, what the hell.'

'What the hell,' agreed the man. Tom was starting to like him.

'The funny thing about that limo,' Tom went on, 'is that I keep seeing it. It's been circling the block all night.'

'Probably looking for parking. Must be murder parking those big boats.'

This struck Tom as a depressingly commonplace explanation. 'I guess I never thought about having to park it.'

The man laughed again and slapped Tom on the back. 'No one ever does! See ya buddy.' And he ambled off happily toward The Glass Onion.

Suddenly the pavement rolled a bit, like a boat on restless water. Tom teetered but kept his balance. He looked around to see if anyone else had noticed the phenomenon; no one had. There were so many people. They pressed in on all sides of him, all looking past him as if they couldn't see him, as if he wasn't worth seeing. He felt as if he could disappear. As if these armies in their rubber masks could devour him, absorb him whole, without ever looking at him. He felt small. He wasn't used to it. He crossed the street.

Here was home base, the bar where Molly and the rest of his life sat waiting. He looked toward the window, preparing a smile, thinking that this was the eve of everything, hoping she was looking so he could wave. He stepped on to the kerb and he looked. She was sitting with some other guy. He could see them both in the front window. The guy was talking, Molly was nodding and pushing her glasses into place, the way she always did, the way he'd seen her do a thousand times before. Her hair was starting to swing loose from its pins; a strand of it curled around her ear. He'd left her alone too long.

Tom stopped. Warm bodies squeezed past him. He stared down at the kerb, thinking that if everything was messed up he had only himself to blame. He'd been too slow. He told himself he'd never done enough.

THE MAN WITHOUT A TEAM

UNCLE ALEC WASN'T DEAD yet.
'Hanging in there,' was how the nurse put it. No, not nurse—hospice worker, carer. I don't know the right word. Soft-soled shoes. I did ask what to call her and she smiled a little and said, 'Lesley.' Which didn't make anything clearer. The place was supposed to feel like a regular house or something. It sort of did, if you ignored the ramps and the overbearing cleanliness and the emergency call button in the loo. Lesley. I'd learned her name four days ago. And Uncle Alec wasn't dead yet.

'Clinging to life, so he is,' said my mother. Her big hands were clasped as if in prayer. Mommy didn't like Uncle Alec much. She said he was useless. Which was a bit rough, but then I'd never found any use for him either. Deathbed vigils were her specialty, though, so she wouldn't waste the opportunity. She'd found out Lesley's name and found out where the tea bags were kept. With these two pieces of information she was unstoppable, queen of the dayroom in less than a week.

I wouldn't go in to see him.

They each passed by—Mommy, Aunt Jean, all the cousins, Uncle Will—on their way to Alec's room. Sometimes they'd try to make me go down the corridor with them.

'He wants to remember Alec the way he was,' explained my mother. Which had nothing to do with it. I had no plans to remember Alec at all. But this was a nice gloss to put on it, this remembering thing. Mommy said it two or three times a day and sometimes it'd take me a minute to remember the "he" was me. Good at gloss is Mommy.

Uncle Will, with his watery gaze, his eyebrows that needed trimmed. The funny corkscrew curl that lay limp on his forehead and spoke of an earlier age. Quite the stud was Will in his day. There are photos of this. Cigarette dangling from the lower lip photos. Now Will moved cautiously, his giant arms marked with the shadows of old bruises, ancient knocks. He was speaking, to me I think—

'Say goodbye to him, John. We owe him that much.'

Where was that sexy cigarette smoker now?

'Are you scared, is that it, lad? It's not so bad. He don't look so bad.'

That was a lie. Alec had lost several stone, his hair was gone and he looked like a caved-in melon the last time I'd seen him, and that was before the hospice.

Cousin Kitty was crying. Big green tuba sounds coming from the corner chair.

***

Back home in Galway I walked at night, gazed into lit windows. I saw families laughing, fighting, eating dinner in the light of the telly. I watched cold clouds, geometric trees dancing on my side of the glass. I knew I belonged where I was. Outside.

***

Kitty had everyone circling around her, offering hankies and cups of tea. They approved of this, this reckless storm of grieving. Kitty got divorced two years ago and her husband got the kid. A little boy. The husband claimed Kitty was unstable. He moved away with the lad and that was that. I remember I liked the boy. He was a quiet sort of lad and he liked trains. Which is not important now.

I felt sorry, okay? I did. For all the good that does.

'I was his favourite,' sobbed Kitty. 'Uncle Alec always said I was his favourite. He'd always pat my hair and give me sweets. He was a star.' No one mentioned that we'd slid into the past tense. 'He was just a lovely wee man. Oh!' She gave in to tears again. Mommy held her hand. For a minute I had the weird idea they were posing for a photo.

Aunt Jean, cardiganned, arms hugging her body. Alec's wife. (Widow—we try the word on like a special-occasion hat.) Mommy forced cups of tea on Jean, her baby sister, and Jean stared at a big circle of empty space...maybe at a clock face visible only to her, ticking off the minutes. I started to feel like this one room, this dayroom in a hospice in Belfast, was the universe. The rain contributed to that impression—all outdoors looked smeared and tremulous. Here was the only solidity. Here amongst tea and television.

Grief had left Jean with no words. She only made barnyard sounds now. Soft lowing, an occasional cluck. I found this so beautiful I almost couldn't stand it. It hurt my eyes like pure light, like a chink in the curtain between banality and something else. Something animal and perfect.

***

In Galway I am a man without a team. A Belfast man in the Republic, a Protestant amongst Catholics, a man who believes in nothing amidst students and drum-makers and girls who sell things in jars in the market, who all believe in everything. Sun-gods and water-sprites and talking Celtic stones. A soft place is Galway. And I am not soft.

Cormac and me met at the factory. Sometimes on Saturday afternoons we'd drink beer together. We had this old man's pub in Woodquay where we liked to go. Cormac's girlfriend would ring his mobile about three times in three hours and eventually he'd slide off home to her. I'd sit on the grass by the boathouse then, watch pensioners feeding the ducks until the sky turned from pigeon-feather grey to a teeth-baring darkness and the wind pushed at my back.

We could talk shite for Ireland, Cormac and me. About our bosses and what was in the paper and any old thing. You wouldn't know what we'd cover in these sessions. The only thing sure was that we gave everyone a rough ride. Contempt was what we had in common. Cormac was one of these silent laughers. He'd lean forward and exhale and his whole long body would gather itself in shudders of mirth. We had a lot of laughs together.

One afternoon he arrived all flushed after a fight with the girlfriend. Some brouhaha over going to visit her mother in Athlone. He ordered tequila; he was lining up the shots and I was suddenly aware of my pulse ticking in my neck. We did the shots. I felt like I was inside one of those snow globes Mommy collects and some big hand was shaking it hard. Wee bits of matter, the stuff of the universe just flung up and spun in the air right in front of me. God it was gorgeous.

Cormac's face went soft with the drink, like a balloon with a slow leak. He was looking at his fingers like they belonged to someone else. 'She doesn't know the first thing about me,' he said. 'After all this time she doesn't understand the way I see my life. My *approach* to life. She doesn't have one! So I'm the bad guy because I have an approach? Because I have principles?'

I didn't know what he was on about. But I rushed to let him know that he was not the bad guy. No fucking way. 'You're good, you're so-o-o good.' I hadn't the vaguest notion what I was on about either. The words weren't words, they were musical notes. There was music. I heard music.

Cormac's instrument squeaked and groaned. I could smell his sweat. 'Women,' he said, looking suddenly at me, 'don't make any sense. Do they? They just go from thing to thing; they have no *plan*, no *approach*. It's not our fault, is it?'

I assured him it wasn't our fault, whatever "it" was and added, 'Women! Who needs 'em?'

'Not us,' agreed Cormac. He put his hand on my shoulder. His fingers dented me. I wanted to suck on him like a sweet.

I rested my hand on his thigh. He leaned forward until I could see his pores. Laughing, he was laughing, silent, strong and I thought I could see the future. I brushed my lips against his. I felt him breathe into my mouth. The music poured out of us, honey gold and thick. Then he scrambled to his feet.

He stared at me. I was scalded. He grabbed his jacket and staggered out. It was like a piece of me ripped away. I was red and raw and visible and I scurried to the door a second later. I threw up into the river. I wished I had the courage to drown.

You know the rest. I took a sick day Monday and Cormac rang me. *Boy were we drunk*, he said. *Can't remember what the hell we talked about. Can't remember anything*, he said. *Yeah*, I said. *Yeah*. After that he and the girlfriend got engaged and his Saturdays were eaten up by meetings with the wedding planner.

You know how it is, he said.

Yeah, I said. Yeah.

***

On day five of the deathbed vigil I announced I was going home. No one tried to dissuade me. I had a job to get back to after all. Jobs are allowed to decide these things for us. Anyhow, Alec was still dying—the old fecker—in no more or less of a hurry than he had been when I arrived. I wasn't contributing much to the proceedings, you have to admit. So I could go.

Except I couldn't let myself leave. I stood in that cold blue corridor and stared at the white door at the end. I don't know how long I stood there. The thought came to me that if I ever wanted to be transformed from this painted wood into a real boy, Alec's room was a place to start. Maybe if I made myself look at that pudding of purple veins and sagging yellow skin. If I braved the smell of decay and old man's wind and murmured the proper platitudes about how he was looking well and when were they going to let him out of here? I don't know. Maybe then I could start to live.

My bus sat hunkered on the kerb outside Connolly Station for a century or two, myself squeezed and bent into a seat—I'm bloody tall, I never fit right. My head leaned against the window and I watched a brown Walkers' crisp packet, kited by the wind, sail lazily down the footpath. I envied its progress. Some sort of match had just ended at Croke Park. I knew this because the bus was crowded with men and boys carrying flags and talking loudly. Some wore red jerseys, some blue. You knew some sort of tribal event had happened because the blue men were delighted with themselves and the red men walked with heavy feet. 'They got *walloped*,' one of the blue men told me. He was laughing, his breath made clouds. The doors were left open and inside the bus it was freezing.

I thought about Alec. Yeah, I finally did it, finally went in that door. He was sleeping when I looked in. All alone. It was funny, after all the build-up, just an old man in a bed, sleeping. A shrunken figure draped in a thin white cover, sprawled in perfect ignorance, a sparkle of drool on his chin. I just stood there; there was nothing else to do. I couldn't make a big goodbye speech or anything corny like that. All I did, I watched his eyes. They were fluttering and darting under thin red lids. Dreaming. It felt like a tease. I wanted to know what he was dreaming about. Now, on the bus, I pressed my cheek to the window and thought about Alec on the threshold of death. Thought that in a way Alec had his faced pressed against a window too. Was it as cold as this? What could he see through it? Did angels dance like crisp packets across Alec's sky?

Suddenly the motor cleared its throat and engaged. The two teams of men sat back in their seats. So did I. The doors sighed shut and the bus pulled away from the kerb.

EARTH-BOUND PEOPLE

5:58 am

SUDDEN BLOOD RED LIGHT. Her fingers on your arm. You feel the bones clutching. 'I'm sorry.'

Straight-jacketed by too-heavy blankets, you don't move. A car horn, somewhere. 'I wanted to tell you I'm sorry.' Curtains. The curtains make the light red. Blink.

Your mother's words are bloated like pills, swallowed and vomited and swallowed again. Losing their shape.

'Do you forgive me?' Her voice is too close, a feeling as much as a sound. A disruption of molecules. 'I'm trying to say I'm sorry.'

You wonder what is called for.

2:09 am

In the lamplight she looks raw, again. The couch is a forgiving shade of beige and the lamp terra cotta. Fat. The coffee table is green glass, unkind. She is puddled on the couch. She has been crying. Again. You notice this and the phone cord stretched, beseeching, and all this rawness makes you sick and embarrassed; you hope you can get to the stairs and up. You focus on the banister with all your will, as if you could pull it closer with your eyes. You look only at the banister, brown and white. But after all there is no way out. The clatter of the unkind coffee table as she puts her glass down. Again.

'Deirdre?'

You turn and say, 'What? Hi Mom,' as if you have just seen her there. The banister recedes.

'Aunt Jane wants to talk to you.'

This is new. 'Hello Aunt Jane,' you say when the phone is passed to you. It's two in the morning, all the adults have lost their minds and you say in your sunniest voice, 'Hello Aunt Jane. How are you?'

'Oh *Dee*,' she says. 'I'm glad you're home.' What will you say if she asks where you were? But she doesn't ask. 'Listen Sugar, I think your mom needs our help. That bastard Ronnie—excuse my language, but you're a teenager now, you're old enough to know. That bastard's let her down again. What does she expect? Lie down with dogs—anyway. She's taking it bad. You know your mom.'

'Yes.'

'The poor thing! I don't want you to worry. She's licking her wounds, that's all. She'll be back to her old self soon as she gets some sleep.'

She doesn't sleep. You've heard her roaming the house at all hours. Water running. Sinatra.

'She's been drinking, Sugar. You probably figured that out?'

'Yes.'

'Okay. Here's what you do. You see the bottle of Jack anywhere? Is it on the coffee table?'

'No.'

'Kitchen table, maybe?'

'Yes.' Brown, broad-shouldered. A joke your mother makes: Jack Daniels, man of the house. 'Here's what you do. Give the phone back to your mom, and while she's talking to me you're gonna pour the Jack down the sink. Understand? She's had enough. We're going to remove the temptation.'

You've always looked after her. Now they want to phone you up and *tell* you to look after her? What do they think you are, a kid?

You hand the phone back to your mother, who sucks on a cigarette in the lamplight. She is wearing a flower-print housecoat your dad gave her. You have vowed a sacred vow never to ever wear a flower-print housecoat when you are an adult. No matter how bad things are. You will always have "outfits", like Nicki's mom. Not a blouse and skirt but an "outfit". And your nails always done and Belle Noir eyeliner. You have plans.

You hand the phone to your mother and she stabs out her cigarette and says, 'Thank you.'

Her voice is hoarse and snuffly like she has a cold, with a vein of prim girlishness that makes you picture her for a second as a girl; a small girl with dull brown hair, her hands clasped behind her back, and a dull hopeful expression. You blink the picture away because you feel so sorry for that girl. She didn't know anything. You feel very old as you step back. You hear your mother say 'Jane?' like a creaky hinge and you go to the kitchen table.

Your mother hates the table. You don't mind it. Sparkly gold dots like fireworks melting in a white Formica sky. The metal edge feels greasy. The chairs are black with gold dots, the piping on the seats starting to unravel. Your mother's been folding down corners of catalogue pages so you know this table's days are numbered. One day you'll come home to a Dinette Set, heavy and frowning like the coffee table. But for the rest of your life, when anyone says "kitchen table", the speckled Formica is what you'll picture. With the white plastic Great Lakes napkin holder dead centre.

The next phase of the operation must be carried out quickly and smoothly. Hiccupy hesitations could give the game away. You lift the bottle, and without a backward glance, you head into the kitchen. Mom is telling Jane about Ronnie's smile, "Like diamonds...like goddamn Burt Reynolds.' She's sort of laughing and you laugh too.

Cereal bowls and a Pyrex dish in the sink. A damp oniony smell and waxy-white drippings of melted cheese floating in oily water. You slide the dishes to one side.

'Like a million bucks, I'm telling you, he really looked the part.' The top is off. At first you just enjoy the scent, honey and smoke, and then you tip the bottle and Jack curls down the drain. 'That's easy for you to say, Jane.' You turn on the tap and splash some water against the back wall of the sink. 'And I'm supposed to sit here alone, night after night? I'm supposed to—'

You chuck the bottle in the garbage.

Rub your hands dry on your jeans. You got away with it. You could be a secret agent. 'G'night Mom,' you call out. Ambling up the stairs now. All innocence.

'*Deir*-dre?' Her voice flails like an animal caught in a trap.

Damn it. 'Yeah?' Halfway up the stairs.

'Dee...' You *have* to turn around and look. She is a dropped doll. The receiver in a wilted hand. 'Dee, where are you going?'

It's as if she's grabbed your ankle and is pulling you down. 'To bed, where do you think?' Stupid fucking question! You'll be up for school in five hours. "Where are you going?" means "stay". She's pulling you down. 'Go to sleep, for Chrissake,' you say. Her miserable cow-eyed face. You hate this, hate the withering voice that comes out of you, hate yourself because it's like slapping an infant. Nicki's mom says, 'Don't you DARE talk back to me!' and the dog hides under the couch. But your mom doesn't say that. Your mom just takes it.

You stomp up the stairs and slam your bedroom door; but it's fake, you're a fake. Pretending to be the age you are when inside you feel much older. You can't understand how life keeps happening. Without a pause. There's no way to hit the brakes, cry uncle, make it stop. Life just keeps happening.

12:32 am

Free.

Nicki's hair is orange under the streetlights and her face is pale and smooth like a mask. Her eyes are panther eyes, lined in Belle Noir eyeliner. She's taught you how to do that, how you hold the tip of the liner pencil over a flame until it's soft and then apply it to the lower lid, extending the line past the outer corner of the eye. Belle Noir. Beautiful, beautiful night.

The swing pendulums down and up. Down and the asphalt glitters; up and the sky hums. The sky has depth, you could drown up here. Earth-bound people have no idea.

Nicki sings. *Put on your red shoes and DANCE...* Her voice is throaty and you have the feeling anything could happen.

Bowie is the man. So beautiful, his eyes so wise and you shiver all over just looking at him. Nicki wants to fuck him. She talks about it all the time. You just want him to look at you, scalding you like the hot black tip of the liner pencil with his stare. That's enough. You listened to *Heroes* tonight while you smoked the first bowl, and when he sang about being heroes forever, you felt he was talking to you. Nicki called you a sappy wench. Nicki has hard muscled arms and a compact little body. When she calls you wench, it's thrilling.

You moved like outlaws through the night. Past the corner boys in front of De Luca's store, who ring around you saying, 'Show us some titty, Baby.' On your own you huddle down into your jacket, hands in pockets and chin on chest, trying to disappear. But with Nicki when you're stoned you pass through the boys like lightning, giggling like crazy. Spilling down 26st Street. Your flash blinds them.

You smoke another bowl when you get to the playground. Cross-legged on the flesh-coloured rubber mat under the monkey bars. No wind. The flame spreads eagerly. The smoke sinks into you. Every particle of you expands and is grateful.

You drop into the middle swing, the chains cold on your fingers. You kick your legs out into nothing. You remember being small, your mom hoisting you up into the swing. You in your too-big galoshes and fat coat with the fur-lined hood. She'd pretty much toss you up into the seat—'hold on now Deirdre'—and then step back. Sometimes she'd start you swinging. But what you remember is her stepping back, her eyes on you, and then past you and away. Somewhere where trees met sky. And she wasn't Mother then. She was Someone Else, with no daughter. She was small and cold in her thin corduroy jacket and the wind lifted her hair and drew it across her face. And she flickered like a candle and you knew for a moment that she *could* just walk away from you, and you were as scared as you have ever been.

Maybe she should have. Walked away. Maybe one of you should. But though you have seen how she looks without you, you don't know yet how you look without her. Belle Noir eyeliner and Nicki's arms around your waist. Scraps of clues as to who you might be. Some day. When there's room.

Hold on now, Deirdre.

When the swing reaches the top of the arc, you are hung like a moon over trees and river and the lights in the distance, the glittering necklace of cars on the Expressway. You see that your world is not the only world, and you're glad and scared and humbled and relieved. There is more than this.

Earth-bound people have no idea.

6:04 *am*

Perched on the edge of your bed, she lists her crimes in a wire-thin voice. Sorry. For Lloyd, who spent all our money. For Mickey, who pinched your behind on your twelfth birthday. For Ronnie, who drinks, who makes me drink, who's left us now like the rest of them. Sorry for being the kind who gets left. Why do they? Why am I?

You slither out from the covers. You sit beside your mother and hold her hand. Right now there is no more than this.

And the night contracts. Another blood red day.

FONDLY

IT WAS THE SONG that did it. She was standing behind the counter, steaming milk in a metal pitcher, when above the whoosh and hiss of the steam she heard it. Suddenly in front of her eyes was the pattern of his duvet, the navy and pale blue squares, and the scent of sandalwood incense drifting above the staleness of his parents' house that was closed tight like a fist against winter. She felt the bed shiver as he shifted in his sleep. She saw her own fingers stroke the warm, creased skin on the back of his neck.

Then the song ended, replaced by the noon Angelus, returning Kate to the world of the Apostasy Café. She shut off the steam, wiped the nozzle and slammed the pitcher on the counter to drive the air bubbles from the milk. In her mind's eye he was posing in his wood-panelled bedroom. Hip cocked, black hair dishevelled. A flash of white teeth when he smiled. A pure, pulsing energy underneath his sallow skin that caused him to look like he was springing forward even when he was perfectly still. Grinning in front of the black and white poster of Bob Dylan. A cigarette dangled from Dylan's down-turned mouth. The letters on the poster read *Don't Look Back*.

It was going to rain. Kate decided while the café was quiet she would grind more coffee in case there was a rush. Rain was good for business.

Maybe he would come in today. Wearing that same old blue and white jersey. Surprised to see her—no, not surprised. He was never surprised. But, pleased. Maybe he would kiss her hand? His lips would feel cold. He would say, 'What a miraculous coincidence!' Or something with less syllables that meant the same thing. She would explain that it was not a coincidence. She would remind him of the letter, the only letter he had sent her since moving to Galway. She would repeat for him the first sentence: *I am sitting in a place called the Apostasy Café, sipping a chai latte and thinking, fondly, of you.* Maybe if he had not used the word "fondly" she would not have packed her belongings and followed him west from Rathdowney. But he had, and so of course she did. In the dust-grey stillness after he had gone, she had warmed herself by thinking of him, thinking fondly of her at a table by the window in a colour-filled place called the Apostasy Café.

Mutual friends were no help in locating him. He was not listed in the phone book either. She had taken to wandering the crowded streets. Every time she turned a corner she expected to collide with him. She actually braced herself for the blow, but her body hit nothing but empty air. When she reached for a bunch of grapes at Teresa's Fruit Stand, she expected his hand to descend at the same moment. He loved grapes. When she crossed Eyre Square she would eagerly scan the faces of the drunks and skateboarders, looking for his dark, complacent eyes. Sometimes on her break she would sit by the canal with its greeny-brown water and skeletal glimpses of submerged shopping trolleys. She would feed the swans and wonder if he had ever fed them. A pale line of seagulls would sail by overhead. Kate would wonder if they had flown over him, too.

The coffee was ground and measured into filters. She washed the grit from her hands. Outside all was strangely still under the woolly, swollen sky. She stood in the doorway and tilted her head upwards, praying for rain to brush her face, wet her mouth, trickle down her neck.

Nothing.

She closed her eyes and floated effortlessly back to another afternoon, a rare scorcher. Heat glittered like silver dust in the air. Her head was cradled in his lap. Blades of grass scratched the backs of her legs. She had shut her eyes against the white summer light.

I am sitting...

Drops of water had landed on her face. Like the drumming of tiny fingers. She had opened her eyes, surprised that rain could come on so suddenly.

I am sitting in a place...

It wasn't raining. He had doused his head with cool water from their thermos and was cheerfully shaking out his hair over her face, creating the soft drizzle she had felt. She had opened her eyes and seen his face inches above hers, the tanned skin crinkling around his gleeful eyes. He was a rare, honey-skinned boy, all ambers and browns. The flash of white teeth like snow on baked ground. Or lightning. His face filled her eyes.

I am sitting in a place called the Apostasy Café...

The rain began begrudgingly. The sky was a woman who had cried too often, until even her tears were tired.

I am sitting in a place called the Apostasy Café...and thinking, fondly, of you.

GRACE

MISS SAID HE BLED through seven bandages before the doctor came. I can still hear him shrieking, a nasty sound, the sound of a cat with its tail on fire. I still hear the laughter. Mrs R.'s crone cackle and her with bits of her brother's flesh still stuck between her teeth. No shame at all. I imagine that's the best thing about going mad; no longer feeling sorry for anything. Mr Mason should have known better. He knows how she gets. But he would go leaning over her, his shoulder just above her nose—'Oh, my poor sister, my poor dear sister!'—so busy blubbering he never noticed her baring her teeth.

That was last night. They've all gone now, thank Heaven—Mr Mason, the doctor, Mr Rochester and Miss Eyre. It is morning and they've all gone back to the sunlit parts of the house. I'm feeding Mrs R. her porridge. She's sitting up in bed, calm as you please, opening her mouth like a good girl. She is very good sometimes, though no one ever sees that but me. I'm thinking I might try to trim her hair today. It's always a risk, coming near her with the scissors. But she's quite relaxed today; a taste of human meat does seem to pacify her. I'd like to get her hair out of her eyes, neaten the line in the back.

Breakfast over, I pile our dishes on a tray for one of the maids to collect. I turn and stoke the fire. Its heat on my skin is welcome; our attic rooms are so chilly and dim. My eyes stray to the mirror above the dressing table. 'Just as I thought,' I say to Mrs R. 'Mine's nearly as bad as yours. Haircuts all round then.' She makes a funny groan, like wind in a chimney. That's her way.

I am singing to myself as I unlock the bottom dresser drawer and lift out the soft parcel. *Rock of Ages, cleft for me—* I fold back the protecting cloth. That familiar cold glint. *Let me hide myself in thee—*They have waited for me. My mother's sewing scissors, heavy now in my hands. The finger grips like open mouths. The shank like a woman, arms above her head, balancing on tiptoe. Her bosom, her legs tapering to two sharp points. I've left off singing. The silence hammers against my ears as I reassure myself the blades are clean. No wiry hairs, no gristle, no stains. I do this every time. And when I'm sure there's nothing I always have to blink and rub my temple and remind myself where I am now. How much time has passed. And I'm never sure if I'm glad or sorry that there is no evidence left.

Too much quiet; I start singing again. *Rock of Ages, cleft for me, let me hide myself in thee. Let the water and the blood, from thy wounded side which flowed...*I shake my head and the terrible pictures fade. I see instead Mrs R. in the bed, her lips twisted into what I think is a smile. This is her favourite hymn. And mine. *Be of sin the double cure—* and I smile back at her, my fingers tight around steel. *Save from wrath. And make me pure.*

My mother called me Grace because she saw God's grace shining like a soft light from my features. Our mothers see things in us no one else can. She was a mild sickly woman, my mother, and I know that God sent me to look after her. I know that He gave me these strong shoulders and this stout heart so I could be of help to her and all the seven children she bore after me. I know He made me ugly so no man would take me from her.

But Grace is a soft whisper of a name and as a girl I always seemed to be arriving just behind it, lumbering and flushed, with the thundering stride of some beast of the fields let into the house by mistake. A plain, earthy name would've suited me better. I hated being Grace, because I could never be Grace, however hard I tried.

'Never mind,' my mother would say. I would rest my cheek on her knee and she'd put down her sewing and stroke my tangled ginger curls.

No one's touched me with such tenderness since.

'Never mind,' she'd say. 'You *are* Grace, whether you see it or not. Think you that God makes angels' wings out of faith alone? Silly girl! Not only faith but ferociousness is needed, if one is to fly. And fly you will, my Angel. Mark me, you will. Because you, Grace, are ferocious!'

'But I don't *want* to be ferocious. I want to be soft and kind, like you.'

She would lift up the sewing scissors then. 'Sheffield steel,' she would say with pride. Mother's kin were from Sheffield. I had a sort of an idea of the place—bustling and loud, dim with factory smoke. Far from our small sea-side parish. I had a child's notion, from Mother's stories, that Sheffield was peopled with noisy, red-haired giants. 'These are made of Sheffield steel and so are you,' she would whisper, putting the scissors down and tapping me on the nose. 'Be glad of it. Providence has His plans, Grace; but the longer I live the more I feel that the good Lord helps those who are willing to help themselves.'

I was nineteen when Mother died. I missed her so much. It was an ache that followed me through my day. I lost myself in work; feeding the little ones, bathing them, getting them to sleep. When they cried for her I cuddled them and cried too, our sobs coming together like one sound. There was nothing just mine anymore.

When work was done I used to go on rambles, just myself, with only God and the sea for company. No pastors to tell me I must speak softer, tread lighter. No aunties spitting on their hankies and scrubbing at my face. No father calling me Horse, Dog, Witch and banging me about. I would hear God's voice in the rumble and hiss of the waves. Telling me that He alone loved me.

Late at night the children and I would hear *him* stumbling into the cottage. I'd lie awake in the dark and listen to his thumps and scratches and muttered curses in the next room. The same way you'd listen to rats scurrying behind walls and know that the infestation is growing. Know that soon you'll have a river of rats underfoot, squealing and biting. Like that, I lay awake listening to the broken sounds and knowing. And what could I do? What poison could stop a rat that big?

Nothing just mine anymore. He took it, all of it, one night while God and the world were sleeping. Even the voice I pleaded with didn't sound like mine. Hair, arms, mouth, breath, womb, belly, tears, breasts, feet, fingers, blood. When he left me I was a speck of self inside a white stranger's body. And he came back the next night.

Horse. Dog. Witch. Each morning I hurried to hide the signs from my brothers and sisters. I put a damp cloth between my legs. I stood straight, though it hurt to do it, and clothed over the bruises. I shivered with the cold that closed over me like water. I realised I was dead.

The scissors make hungry baby-bird sounds and straight, soft black hairs drift in clumps to the floor. Mrs R. sits straight in her chair. She hasn't much choice, as I've tied her to it. No sense taking risks. She bucked like a stallion when she felt the rope against her arms. But I held on.

'Sheffield steel,' I tell her, pointing to myself. 'Descended from a race of ginger giants. You've no chance against me.'

She has her chin on her chest now. She's breathing deeply and noisily through her nose. I'm doing the back first. Comb and snip, comb and snip. Both of us soothed by the sounds, the touch. Our breath coming together now. Comb and in, and snip and out.

Of course I'm only teasing her when I say she has no chance. She has every chance, for she is mad and has a monstrous strength. She will best me one day, I have no doubt, kill me...it makes me laugh to think of it. It's not that I wish to die, especially. It is that we are, both of us, dead already—good as, anyway—kept away from "gentle folk" by a set of stairs and a locked door. For ones who live as we do, what is it to die?

Important, though, that it not happen *yet*. I need another year. One more year at this wage (and it's a good wage, mind; so it should be!). After that God can do what He likes with me. My duty will be done.

I move to the front of Mrs R. She closes her eyes, peaceful. I bring the scissors to her brow and feel her flinch at the cold blades. She is quite still, but there is tension in it now, a tautness of muscle and nerve. Then she opens her eyes. They are large and brown and now we are eye to eye, two killers sharing a cage.

I trim the hair away from her eyes, blow softly on her face to remove strays. She purrs at me. I chuckle. And now we are mother and daughter.

Mother. I remember the sky hanging heavy and white on that last day. Days like that are remembering days, so my mother used to say. So I walked and I remembered her. And the sky was thick with souls like hers, waiting to ascend into Heaven. The path curved so I could see the sea, the only thing moving. So I went to it. I remembered all the times God had spoken to me in the waves. But God had nothing to say now. And I wondered why He had nothing to say to a girl who just wanted her mother.

I took off my shoes and my dress. I don't know how I felt. Cold. Relieved, I suppose. It would be over soon.

I'd gone about it all wrong, of course. I realised, as I waded in, that a fully-dressed person would sink faster. As well as that, I was a strong swimmer and had trouble telling my limbs to be still when they twitched with desire to carry me through the water. I tried, anyway—kept ducking my foolish head under the green waves, the cold a shock on my scalp, my hair spreading like rays around my face...only to cling miserably to my cheeks when I surfaced again, gasping, spitting, furious. Alive. Each dunking a baptism bringing me back to life. I screeched like a gull.

God was not through with me yet. I peeled off my shift and swam as fast as I could. Heat returned to my fingers and toes. I was half-mad, an animal, thrashing and kicking and rising and falling. I don't know how to say what happened next. I felt a sort of joy; it came like a big sun, melting me. Suddenly I was thinking, MY *body*, MINE. And it was. It belonged to me again. Was it God that made that happen? Or was it Grace?

I swam and swam until my mind was quiet. I had not realised how much noise there was inside my head. I let the water hold me; my eyes were full of grey-white sky. I could feel my heart pounding, hear my own breath. I asked myself, why am I still here? Give me a reason, I begged of God. My lips fell open, my fingers too, my hands floated palms up, waiting to receive the gift He would bestow. A purpose, a shining purpose. If He had continued silent, what pain! Without a plan life is only suffering. I could not die, yet could not have lived. Hell is the in between, the on-and-on, no end in sight, no idea what it's all for. I tell you, I could not bear it.

But just as I felt lost, God found His tongue. Or did I find my ears? Salvation came in a whisper, heard both outside and inside my head. Six words lifted me, brought me safely back to shore.

Go home. The children need you.

Need me! I tugged my dress on, scraped wet hair from my face, strode barefoot up the hill. How often I had taken this path at this hour, thinking to wake Annie, the baby, from her nap and start the evening meal. That routine, that person seemed far from me now. Under the heavy sky the grass and tangled shrubs were blue. The cottage waited beyond the bend. But it was different too. The fire was out; no wisps of smoke from the chimney. No children playing outside. Every stone, every pane of glass in the windows looked cold and secretive. This was no home. I could not make it one.

My thoughts, if you could call them thoughts, danced wild and naked as flames. I hurried inside. And there was the most ordinary sight. Peter and John, playing with blocks on the floor, while under the window sat Lucy. She was mending our father's breeches, a frown of concentration on her face. Lucy was fifteen then and the image of our mother, for whom she was named; small and pale, with shining black hair. She's handy with a needle, always was, not like me with my thick clumsy fingers.

She looked up at me. 'Fire's gone out.'

I nodded dumbly.

'Why is your hair all wet?'

'Gracie, I'm hungry,' said Peter. 'John too.'

'Stop annoying her when she's only in the door! Make yourself useful, can't you?' Lucy laid her mending down and got to her feet. 'Find James. Get that coal bucket filled. Take Snivelly Drawers with you.'

Snivelly Drawers, Christian name John, let out a wail. Peter kicked him in the shin and the howl got louder.

'OUT!' shouted Lucy. Peter obeyed, dragging John and bucket behind him. In the next room Annie woke with a cry.

'See what they've done! I'll get her.' Lucy rushed into the back room.

I stood there with my mouth open like a right silly cow. Couldn't get my head around it—the way everything was the same. Me having thoughts of death and God and what-is-the-purpose, and here they were sewing and fetching coal and walloping each other like it was any other day. It just goes on, life, doesn't it? Like a well-wound clock. It ticks on, not caring what we think of it.

And I was standing there, thinking about life, and I heard Lucy clucking at Annie, and Annie's crying ceased. Then I heard another voice say, 'You're so like your mother.'

He said it softly, like he was musing on it, and she gave a nervous laugh. Then I heard the creak of his chair and I knew he had stood. There was a long moment, during which I could not move, and then there was another sound. A sudden intake of breath. And I knew. I knew before I got to the doorway, my legs finding strength again. I knew before I saw them, I knew it as well as if it was my breast he was cupping, my breath trapped in my throat, my eyes big and staring into his and seeing...seeing.

And I understood then that life does tick on, that if I wasn't there the same things would happen, but they would happen instead to Lucy. And after Lucy, May. And after May, Ruth. And after Ruth, Annie. It wouldn't stop. My death wouldn't stop it. Only one death could.

The children need you.

I took the sewing scissors off the bench where Lucy had left them. He turned as I came up to them, turned his pathetic face to me with his hands still on my sister. 'Grace?' he said. And his eyes were full of me then. I remember it with a sort of pride. Because he did not say Horse, Dog, Witch. He called me by my name. It was the first time, I think, he really saw me.

'Grace?'

'Yes, Father,' I said. And I stuck the scissors into his thick yellow neck.

I am looking for the sea.

I can just make it out if I stand here by the easternmost window and crane my neck and squint. There it is. That low slice of sky that moves, flashes. Silvery light in the distance. Sometimes I just need to know it is still there.

Mrs R. in her chair gives a long sigh and it's like she is sighing for both of us. I turn quickly and put the scissors away. Then I untie her. She sits, her eyes down. 'Go on,' I tell her. 'You're free.' But she stays sitting.

'Go on, silly! I've untied you. See?' I hold the rope out but she doesn't look. She doesn't move. Just sits there, all droopy. I perch on the end of the bed. The clock downstairs strikes eleven.

Annie will be wed next year. It doesn't seem possible. He's a ferrety little man, not much to say for himself, but she is soppy over him. He has prospects, so she will be provided for. Please God, she will be happy.

The dress I wore to Ruth's should do for Annie's as well. It's not like anyone will be looking at me, anyway. Our brother James will give her away, May and Ruth will attend her, I will be—a shadow. The grey-faced old maid who keeps her own counsel, who stands at the back and watches to see how her money has been spent. The only one who knows the true cost of everything.

Once you have done murder it is as if a pane of glass comes down between yourself and everyone else. You are different; somewhere between God and mortals with a terrible power in your ordinary hands. I sometimes think that God Himself must feel terribly lonely. No one who understands Him and all those prayers to answer. I think about that every time I go home. Watch all their eyes avoid the sad patch of earth under which James and I planted our father. Oh, they know—everyone knows. Even the Parish Constable knew, and all he said to me was, 'Godspeed, Grace Poole.'

In other words, go. We won't waste a tear on the old bastard, but we'd rather not look on you, either. I make good people uncomfortable. Not the coins I earn, they are comfortable enough with those. But me. Grace was always different, they say. And God bless us, perhaps it had to be done, but had she to do it *like that?* Yes, surely she is not the same as us.

Grace is ferocious.

Forgot my own haircut! Got caught up, didn't I. Those scissors. The sight of them always sends me off. They're the only thing of Mother's I brought with me. And maybe I should be sorry, the way that memories of her always get tangled with memories of that other thing. But I don't think I am sorry. I don't think I mind a bit. Because I think Mother understands and I think she might even be proud of me. I am proud of me. I have to feel some way, so I have decided on proud.

We sit here, Mrs R. and me, and on the other side of the glass the world goes on. Seasons change, men build walls and tend fields, women marry and have babies, and all of it, time, it's moving through my open hands like water.

She will kill me. I see it sometimes just before I fall asleep. See her finally free, and knowing she is free, and coming for me. A vision of Hell, some would say. But to me it is no more than natural, the way things go. Nothing can stay chained forever. Hurt always floats back up to the surface. When it does it makes monsters of us all.

BLOOD LOSS

NOW, IT IS NOW. Almost over.

Sara's hair long and smooth. Not light, not dark. Freckles like nutmeg across her nose. Long-limbed and heedless, everything a nine-year-old should be. Nine, the highest number; after that you're just repeating. May she stay as she is, you think. Nine.

She stands on the back step and watches you through the open door. Sara the watcher. You ask if she's packed for camp. She nods and chews on her lip. Another adult asking boring questions. Then Mrs Lynch descends.

Puts her hands on Sara's shoulder and her hands are pearl-white claws, possessing. Sara-how-many-times-have-I-told-you-don't-bother-the-tenants.

She wasn't, Mrs Lynch. Bothering me.

Did you tell Kate you're off to summer camp today?

Sara nods and spins away, dancing to a tune in her head. The countdown begins. Sara dances like a flame and you call out goodbye across the yard, goodbye, goodbye. She is gone.

Mrs Lynch wonders if you have the rent. Since she is here.

You do, of course you do. Tucked into the inside pocket of your purse. You reach around the door and slip the notes to her. Her fingers brush against yours.

Thanks, Kate.

This has all happened before. Your arms heavy.

A few weeks of peace and quiet before school starts. I can't wait, says Mrs Lynch.

But Sara isn't a noisy child. She is a watcher, silent as a cloud. You suppose that's just something people say. Peace and quiet, mothers are supposed to crave peace and quiet.

Enjoy it, you say, unfolding a smile you have saved for this moment.

Oh I will! says Mrs Lynch, arching her neck in a parody of laughter. Don't you worry! Her face is grotesque, her lips blue in shadow, plump. You try to imagine wanting to kiss them. Someone must have wanted to, once. You can't fathom it. Your knuckles still hum from when her fingers brushed them. It's almost over. Stick to the script. Tell the unkissable Mrs Lynch goodbye.

Now, it is now. You watch yourself make a second cup of coffee. Relief like sunlight, giddy hot relief because it's over; you have lasted and given nothing away.

The decision was reached a week ago and the days have been drizzled with excitement since. Every tiny act was suddenly fat with meaning again. Intent and portent. The last everything. The last film rented, the last sweet and sour prawns. The last *Weekend* Supplement. The last round of errands, pushing the trolley through the supermarket, for once buying just what you wanted, the tastes crowding your mouth...the cellophaned daisies you lifted at the last minute, cold water dripping down your arm at the checkout counter. Standing like a bride with the flowers in your arms, food for an army in your bags. A flash of bliss.

You put everything on the credit card. Let them try to collect from you! You laughed at that, laughed out loud in the car park. Then came to yourself and realised people were staring. Mad woman laughing in the car park. Behave yourself, Kate. If they know what you're up to they won't let you go.

No longer busy. The days were long and silent and you watched the sky parade its colours. Silver-white cracking into blue. Blue deepening like a bruise into purple, green, black. Fierce red dawns. And you stood by the back door and knew there were no more tears, you would not cry again. Your eyes were dry and you saw everything clearly.

Sara. Sara was the only one watching. To the neighbours you were no one. Your mother sent you postcards from her new life. That was all. How had she managed to secure a second life when you hadn't managed to secure even one? Your best friend phones on Saturdays to talk about life in the suburbs, the new husband and his commute, the next door's dog howling at three in the morning and colours of carpet and workmen tracking dirt across the kitchen and she can't get any work done, longs for the barren quiet of an office while the new husband wishes he could work from home. Isn't that always the way? The grass is always greener, etcetera, etcetera. The only character you identified with was the dog, wailing in the darkness. But you didn't say that. It's not that she doesn't care, your friend. She does, but she's busy. And you haven't explained it to her because you don't know how. Words are weak. All you really want to tell her is, I miss you. Come back from your future and visit me here. But you can't say things like that.

Mrs Lynch is dry as chalk, no point in telling her. The café has been sold on; it's an Internet place now. So you have no more work mates. You have no more work. Despite many interviews. Despite photocopied references and your charcoal skirt ironed and your eager smile, which every single interviewer deduced was false. So much for that. Unable to fool anyone, you stayed at home. The corridors of your mind emptied.

But there was Sara. Sara in the utility room, Sara at the back door, Sara on the steps. Silent Sara watching. You couldn't say she'd been a comfort, exactly. Twisting a lock of hair around her fingers and biting her lip. Spinning in place. Smiling without showing any teeth. She was a presence, that was all; she noticed everything. That was why you couldn't do it until she left. Because she might see. She might find the body, witness blood. You couldn't risk it. You couldn't reward her attention that way.

Decapitate the percolator. Shake out the grounds. Methodical. Leave the place tidy.

There is no heaven. You don't want that. Heaven would have its own etiquette, local slang, street names you would have to learn. Death is not supposed to be like moving house. Death is death, the end. A rest. You just need everything to stop.

Steam rises from the sink. Hiss and heat. You've never minded tidying up. You used to sing. Used to belt out old ballads, elbow-deep in suds.

When was the last time you sang?

...Bit by bit, it leaked away.

The singing.

The surprises.

In the note you will leave: *It isn't the grief that I can't take. It's having nothing to look forward to.*

The singing.

Rinse the cup and place it upside down on the drying rack. Your funny old hands.

It leaked away, like from a cracked cup.

Turn off the tap.

Funny old hands. Small, with the scar on the left middle finger.

...leaked away. In the blood. And the pain, Jesus, you knew it wasn't normal. So weak, afterwards.

The scar, a thin white ridge the length of your finger. Childhood incident. Part of your topography.

And you felt so stupid because you hadn't known it was there in the first place. Gone before you knew it existed. Your baby, your chance.

He wrote that maybe it was for the best.

The doctor said to stay positive and prescribed iron tablets.

Your baby, your chance.

The scar has kept you company. Part of your topography. You stopped listening then. To anyone. Heard only your own heartbeat, the tides of blood inside you. Cold that year. This year. The sun had no heat in it. Now it is August and you have a plan.

The dishes done, you close the curtains. The curtains are a knobbly orange material. Mrs Lynch must have picked them, because they look like Mrs Lynch, sort of screechy and nervy and bright. You start to get undressed. The house is quiet. Your room is filled with a restless light.

The note—where's the note? Put it on the kitchen table. It isn't actually addressed to anyone. Doesn't matter.

You drop each piece of clothing in the hamper and then close the lid. Pad into the bathroom, floor cool and damp. This has happened before. Run water into the bath.

He wrote that maybe it was for the best.

When the water is the right temperature, you put the plug in. The water makes a lively sound. Like laughing.

This has happened before. All of it—the laughing water, the restless, rust-coloured light. It has happened before and the outcome already decided. There's nothing you need to think about. A sad joy is born inside you, sitting naked on the edge of the tub.

Goodbye Sara-Silent-As-A-Cloud.

You sat once. Silent. On the bottom stair. Nine-years-old, Sara's age, and like Sara, nothing escaped you. Black and white polished tile, Finbar's toenails clackety clack, his shrill bark. The Heneghans, sprawled on a Sunday. And you, the guest, listening.

What brought that to mind? How are you back there again?

The scar. Pale and straight as a frown, seen and not seen for all these years.

It was a Sunday. Claire read comics in her room. Bored with you. You waited for your mother to pick you up. Mrs Heneghan chattered on the kitchen phone, Mr Heneghan read the *Irish Independent* in the living room. Listened to jazz. Giddy racing piano. Brendan frowned over solitaire in the dining room. And upstairs Claire turned pages while Siobhan—fifteen, a figure of infinite mystery—lay on her stomach on her bed listening to the radio and painting her nails sugar-pink. The Heneghans. And you in the front hall, all of nine, waiting and listening, just like Sara.

But not. Without her nonchalance, her veneer. Maybe what's wrong was already wrong, the cup already cracked. How else do you explain it? Sitting on the stair and Finbar toddled towards you. Shiny black, all waggle and yap. Mrs Heneghan called him Baby. He was everyone's darling. You stretched out your hand to pat his cute little rump. You had no pets at home so you weren't quite sure what to do. But you'd been told Finbar liked everyone.

You patted his rump and gave him an affectionate smile. Finbar's head whipped around. There was pain, crushing hot pain and a confusion of blood and barking. The blood was everywhere all at once, webbed across the back of your hand. You sucked in breath. The sound you didn't make has echoed. The scream you swallowed that day you have swallowed every day since.

Finbar liked everyone, but not you. You ran and hid in the bathroom, cold water rinsing blood down the drain, your other hand clenched against the pain. You couldn't let anyone know. That you made Finbar bite you. They'd really be on to you then. Then they'd know what you know now, as you turn off the water, take the razor from its package, slip into the bath. They'd know the cup is cracked.

Almost over.

You lick your lips. The blood sings.

LIVE NUDE GIRLS

THE MISSION DISTRICT, SAN FRANCISCO: We gathered on Guerrero Street. There were twenty-five of us clustering awkwardly along the sidewalk. Since the performance area was only the size of a living room, and there wasn't much backstage space to speak of, the only way to keep the audience out of the final run-through was to lock us out on the street.

'They must be nervous,' a tall bearded man said shyly.

I remembered Laura in the car that morning, threatening to not go on because in the last practice her buttons had stuck and she couldn't get her shirt off fast enough, and all the other strippers had their routines down, and their costumes were more exotic, and *shit, what was she going to do?* The fingers on her left hand counted the buttons on her blouse, over and over again, while her right hand steadied the steering wheel.

At a few minutes after eight the door was opened by a pale woman with pixie-short hair and an enormous smile. She was wearing a silver crop-top with plunging neckline, dark mini, black lace stockings and platform shoes. The silver top shimmered under the streetlights. 'Sorry to have kept you waiting,' she chirped. 'We're ready for you now.' She handed pink programmes to each of us as we filed in.

The room was longer than it was wide. Trixie, the shimmering mistress of ceremonies, chattered welcoming remarks as she fumbled with a boom box in the corner. I sat between a young woman who was busy making out with her heavily tattooed girlfriend, and a barrel-chested man nervously clutching a bouquet of red roses in his fist.

The door to the dressing room was slightly open and out of the crack oozed women's body parts. A leg, an arm, two heads...as though one many-headed, multi-limbed she-beast was caged in the next room. The heads peeked out at the audience, bit their lips and giggled nervously. Fluttering hands tugged on a red stocking top. A leather mini-skirted ass presented and withdrew. I glimpsed hair—black and smooth, red and wispy, brown and coiled, blonde and bluntly short. And skin—chalk, almond, gold.

'The art of erotic dance isn't something that can be taught,' Trixie told the audience. 'It's something that's in all of us.' After only five weeks of instruction the class would strip before an audience for the first time tonight. The women had chosen their own music and, to a large extent, choreographed their own numbers. 'This is *them*,' promised Trixie.

North Beach:

Overcome with curiosity and many martinis, Laura and I snuck into a club in North Beach whose neon sign promised **LIVE NUDE GIRLS**. But inside there was no stage. Instead, there were booths, only slightly larger than phone booths. Inside each one, in the wall opposite the door, was a tiny window through which the customer watched a woman dance. On the floors of the booths were drifts of soiled white tissues.

It was strangely peaceful inside the club, murky and quiet, a place seemingly miles beneath the sea. A skinny Hispanic girl in pasties and a thong was escorted through the halls by what must have been the bouncer, an anaemic, acned teen dressed all in black, who made a great show of protecting the dancer from the clientele. But no one paid her any attention at all. With glittering nipples and a movie-star smile, she glided down the hall in a cloud of something like glamour.

The Mission District:

By the thirteenth routine in the Guerrero Street show, the shock of women getting naked to music just a few feet away from me had worn off; bouncing boobs and butt cracks became as erotic as ceiling tiles, doorknobs, dust motes. But the dancers themselves remained captivating. There were all ages and body types, all kinds of props utilized. One forty year-old wore a sleek black mask over her spectacles. A young, leggy blonde licked a lollipop. One performer wore a dildo strapped into place, and a t-shirt that said "Right tool for the job". Another girl licked whipped cream off the erect dildo.

Some dancers smiled and made eye contact with the audience, while others focussed their attention on their boyfriend or girlfriend. The barrel-chested man beside me received a lap dance from his lover. She writhed against him, eyes gleaming, while he turned red from excitement, embarrassment or both.

Not everything went perfectly. Zippers jammed, pasties fell off. One woman threw off her high heels with abandon and hit a man in the front row. Both she and the man laughed breathlessly. When Laura performed, the troublesome buttons opened with ease, though she slipped from her blouse one chorus too early. It didn't matter, the audience loved her anyway. At the end of her routine, in a roar of applause, she paused for a moment at centre stage and smiled proudly.

The crowd howled, moaned, panted and whistled. One by one, after they danced, the women joined the audience, sometimes without dressing first. Some perched on lovers' knees. Others sprawled in corners, like contented cats. Not a used Kleenex to be seen anywhere.

EVERYONE'S MOTHER

AFTER THE SEX Peg asked Vin to tune in her VCR. She'd heard you get better reception that way. Vin rolled down his window and lit a Marlboro. 'You should get cable.'

'Can't afford it,' said Peg, peeling her rear end off the seat to pull her skirt down. 'Couldn't afford the VCR but Lorene's ex made us a deal.'

'He do car stereos too?'

'Sure. I'll give you his card. What about my VCR?'

'Nothing to it. You want me to go in the house now and do it for you?'

'Better wait till after Labor Day. Mary Denise will be back up at school.'

'Honey,' asked Vin as he squeezed Peg's knee, 'how come your daughter doesn't like me?'

'Aww. Don't take it to heart. Mary Denise doesn't like anybody.'

They were quiet for a while, listening to the car radio. Woven through shards of static was Donna Summer purring 'I Feel Love'. Vin fiddled with the dial but couldn't get the station in any clearer. 'Damn thing,' he grunted. He tossed his cigarette out the window and let his balding head drop against the seat. Soon he was asleep.

He looks like a baby, Peg thought with a quiver of fondness. *Like a helpless baby with grey nose hair.* It was easy to care about him this way, his trousers at his ankles, his shirt unbuttoned to reveal flesh purple-white as a turnip. She ran a flat hand down his chest and belly, the same way she'd smooth a favourite tablecloth. Then she found her bag and started rooting for her lipstick.

The song disintegrated into a sh-h-h. She rolled her window all the way down, closed her eyes and leaned her head out. It was finally dark. The air was almost cool and almost fresh. She pretended the car was in motion, the wind moving through her curls as she and Vin motored toward a city of coloured lights in the distance. She didn't care if they ever got there. It was the travelling, the road, the being nowhere with everything to look forward to. She puckered her lips and tried to take a big sip of night.

If only Vin would wake up and drive them somewhere. Even downtown. Or wake up and just talk to her. She opened her eyes and the street lights on Ringold Street were burning orange, turning everything yellow-brown, like an old photo. Everything was still; it could have been a photo. The radio hissed.

At least in the car she could sort of pretend they were teenagers again; smell of leather, dashboard starlight, sudden cold of a seatbelt buckle under her rear end. There was something fumbly-clean-breakfast-cereal-American about it. Especially as the car was a sedan. Not one of these Japanese tin cans, but a baby-blue four-door Chevy Impala with white interior, first owned by Vin's Uncle Aldo. Got lousy mileage, a bitch to park, and the radio was crummy. But God, what a beauty! Like the cheeseburgers in that diner they liked on 21st Street. Fat, drippy cheeseburgers you had to hold in two hands, with pickle slices and the little cup of coleslaw on the plate. Cheeseburger Deluxe, they called it. *De-luxe*. Peg tried the word out, whispering to herself. It had a square-cut sound. It sparkled.

There used to be more about Philly that was Deluxe, a lot more, but somehow lately everything had gotten all small and stooped-over: cars, food, movie screens. Small and full of apologies. Sometimes she felt she was about to apologise herself to death. Especially when Mary Denise was home from college.

She remembered last Christmas, the fuss over presents. Mary Denise hadn't wanted any. She'd sent all of her Christmas money to the American Indian Movement and wanted Peg to do the same. If all Americans would, she said, there was a chance real healing could take place. She was so serious about it, you wouldn't dare make a joke. Peg herself had never done a thing against an Indian and never would. She just couldn't see what Indians had to do with Christmas.

And then last Easter. Mary Denise had refused to wear a bra to church. She said she didn't believe in bras anymore. What could you say to that? As if bras were like Santa or the Easter Bunny. Now, Peg didn't live in a cave. She knew that bralessness had been a fashion once, years back. But it wasn't the fashion anymore. And she simply did not see why her daughter was so downright smug about the fact that she was standing in God's house with her tits all wibbily-wobbily. Not to mention the lack of makeup and the armpit hair. She'd looked just awful! And she was such a pretty girl. It wasn't that Peg cared what the other parishioners would think—she only went to church twice a year anyway, what did she care what the other parishioners would think? They could mind their own beeswax. No, her worry wasn't people, but the respect that a girl should show for her appearance, for her body. It just wasn't right, showing up for a service half-dressed. Just not right. She had tried to explain this on the way home, and Mary Denise had hit her with this:

'Can I ask you something? All that *God the Father* stuff. Doesn't that bug you at all?'

'Bug me?' Peg stopped walking. 'Why should it bug me?'

'Because they're just assuming that God is a man! Why can't She be a woman? Why can't they say *God the Mother?*'

'Because,' said Peg, 'because, that's not, He isn't, that's not what it is.'

'If we must give the Divinity a gender, why can't it be female? Don't you feel excluded by this patriarchal bullshit?'

Mary Denise was standing in front of Delancey's Drugs, twirling her hair on one finger the way she had as a little girl. The gesture made Peg want to cry. She missed her child. She wanted to lead her by the hand through Delancey's, to the counter where she'd buy her a pack of Bubble Yum. Pink.

'I'm going to lend you some books.' The no-longer-child started walking again, taking long strides. 'As a woman you really owe it to yourself to question this stuff—'

Peg didn't want to question, there was enough to question without adding in God and all they'd taught her when she was Margaret Mary Feeney in white knee socks. And she knew her place in the story. God was God and Mary was God's Mother. Everyone's Mother. Wasn't that good enough?

Maybe she hadn't explained it well enough when Mary Denise was small. There'd been so much else to cover. Eat your carrots, stop picking at that, look both ways, don't take candy from a stranger, sit like a lady. Don't stare at that man, he can't help it. Be kind to your elders.

Sex is for when you're in love. Put that down, you don't know where it's been. Be careful. Be careful, be careful. Don't take candy from a stranger.

*ROXanne...you don't have to wear...*the radio howled back to life. Peg sat up, grinning, started tapping a beat on the dashboard. Vin snorted and opened his eyes.

'He sings like a girl.'

She laughed. 'Fuddy duddy.'

'And proud of it.'

'They're a top ten group, Mary Denise says.'

'Gimme Frank any day.'

There were two framed pictures on the wall of Vin's living room, one of the Pope and one of Sinatra. Peg had often sat there in the half-dark (the heavy front curtains always drawn) and watched dust motes hover like tiny angels around Frank's glass-encased face. She sat very still so the couch's plastic slipcover would not crunch beneath her. Veronica, Vin's mother, spoke mostly Italian, and the tiny black-clad woman could have been delivering the Latin Mass for all Peg could tell. There was that sort of solemn power in her gestures and voice. She always addressed Vin as *Vincente* and the name gave Peg shivers, it was so foreign and romantic. She thought Veronica liked her. It was hard to tell. But mothers had always liked her; she had just enough of that good-Catholic-girl thing going on. She wanted her to like her because Vin absolutely revered his mama in a charming old-world sort of way. And this of course meant no fooling around at all in Vin's house. Veronica had the ears of a bat.

Vin lifted his tush off the seat so he could pull his pants up. 'How long was I asleep?'

'I don't know. Vin, let's go somewhere.'

'You gotta be kidding. Where you want to go?'

'Let's take a drive.'

'Drive where? It's late. I'm beat.'

'Come on! Please?'

'Peggy, for Christ sake. I'm only human.'

'There must be something going on, somewhere.'

He leaned over her and planted a dry kiss on her mouth. 'Something was going on *in here*. And it was nice. Wasn't it nice?'

She sighed. 'Very nice.'

'There you go! It was nice, and now we're going to do what normal people do after the nice and go to bed and get some sleep.'

Normal. That rankled. 'We're not that old, and I do enough normal. We're barely middle-aged.'

'I didn't say old, I said *tired*. Now. Can we go into your place? Everyone's got to be asleep by now.'

'Mary Denise will be up. She's a night owl.'

Vin put his hands up in a gesture of surrender. 'Mary Denise, Mary Denise. Alright. You go in and I'll drive home. Talk to you tomorrow, after I take Ma to church.'

'That's it? You're just going to go?'

'What else can I do? We got your daughter up there, my ma over there, and you and me stuck in the middle, like always. Honey, what else can I do?'

Peg stared at her house across the street. It was a small brick row house—a box in a row of boxes. How could her life be contained in there? She felt bigger than the box. She imagined herself as an immense, shifting cloud that hung over the city and reflected back its lights and wishes.

Peg had never been to college. She had had an idea that Mary Denise would come home full of news of her new best friends, the football player she was dating. Stories of crisp New England nights, glasses of beer on an old whitewashed porch, her boyfriend placing his jacket across her shoulders. Nights where anything seemed possible.

Instead there were Indians. And women in poor countries hoodwinked by baby formula companies. Hypocritical drug laws, pollution in the rain, poisons in the meat. So many victims and Mary Denise bled for all of them. Why? Couldn't she see how very lucky she was? Why was she so angry all the time?

'Alright. Here's a deal.' His voice, low and rumbly and by far the sexiest thing about him. It interrupted her thoughts. 'How about I take my lady out for a soda or something?'

She smiled. *My lady.* That was nice. 'Wow. Big spender.'

'Hey, there's not a lot open this late. Not that we can walk to, anyhow. But a nice little stroll to that 24-hour store on Lombard? That I could do.'

'You're out of cigarettes, aren't you?'

He chuckled. 'And here I thought I was being all smooth.'

She rolled her eyes. 'You are smooth. Smooth as fondue and twice as cheesy. C'mon, let's go.'

He held open her door. She stood smoothing her skirt and he took her hand and led her up on to the sidewalk. She wondered what they would look like to someone passing by. This slim, permed woman in her going-out clothes next to this balding man whose belly hung over his belt. Not an obvious match. But there were no passers-by, the street was empty. Vin took his usual place on her outside to shield her from splashing mud or kerb-jumping cars. But there was nobody, nothing. It was an instinct of his, a bit of useless chivalry. It made her wonder how many things they both did that were empty of meaning. Habit. Mary Denise would be insulted, she knew, would say it was chauvinist, the way he tried to get between her and the big bad world. Peg did not feel insulted, but tired. They turned left on South Street and she thought ahead to herself on Monday, seven in the morning, standing in this same street flagging down the Number 90 so it wouldn't speed past her. Coffee churning in her stomach, the low-fat break-fast bars she had not had time to eat shoved in her purse. Shoes pinching her toes. Tired.

The spell was broken.

She stopped walking. 'Vin?'

He stopped. 'Yeah?'

'I think I changed my mind.' Her throat was suddenly tight. She looked at him and she saw a man doing the best he could. But she didn't see her future.

'So, what? You wanna call it a night?' He stood waiting for directions.

'I do. I wanna call it a night. I'm sorry.'

Vin shrugged. 'That's ok. I'll walk you home.'

And he did. They smooched a little on the top step and he waited while she dug her keys out of her bag. He made his usual little joke about how her handbag was like this black hole into which everything vanished. She laughed a little and felt very sad. Then he left, the Impala's engine rattling in the silence.

Mary Denise was curled up on the couch, watching TV and eating ice cream directly from the container.

'Don't go overboard with that stuff.'

'Hello to you too,' said Mary Denise.

'It gets harder and harder to lose those extra pounds as you get older. Just wait until you're my age.'

'Mother, unlike you, I have no interest in conforming to the media image of an attractive female.'

Peg sighed. 'Okay.'

'Seriously, you do know they airbrush all those magazine photos? It's not real. You're aspiring to something that isn't real.'

'Okay! Take your shoes off my couch.'

Mary Denise groaned and rearranged herself. 'Must have been a great date.'

'It was fine. What are you watching?'

'That movie, you know, with what's-his-name.'

'Lorene go to bed?'

'Yeah. Cliff phoned, so she was in a mood.'

'Oh boy. Was she crying?'

'No, she was dusting. Ten o'clock at night and she was *dusting*.'

'Well, that's how she deals with it.'

'That woman has issues.'

'We all have issues. Be nice.' Cliff was Lorene's ex. Three years ago they had moved up from Shreveport so Cliff could manage his uncle's appliance store out in Upper Darby. He'd settled right into the job and also into an affair with the store's delivery boy, Jason. After a while he had come clean, suggesting to Lorene that Jason could move in with the two of them. *That way we'd all be together*, he'd said hopefully. *Like a proper family.*

Lorene left.

Too ashamed to go back to Louisiana, she'd landed on her friend Peg's stoop in a cloud of White Shoulders and grief. For four days she'd cried her eyes out on Peg's beige loveseat. Now her Oil of Olay lived on the lace runner on top of the dresser in Peg's spare room.

'She was blasting the Johnny Cash records again.'

'She's homesick.'

'Why doesn't she go home if she's so miserable?'

'This is her home.'

'You know what I mean. Back down South.'

'She can't face her family. That's the problem. She doesn't know how to go forward and she can't go back. She's stuck.' Peg swung her leg like a girl. 'Poor Lorene.'

Mary Denise put the ice cream carton down on the coffee table. 'Well you know, it's nice of you. The way you took her in and stuff.'

'It's nothing. Put something under that.'

She moved the *TV Guide* under the dripping container. 'No, I mean, really. It's good. Feminist solidarity. We have to stick together.'

'Thank you.' Peg risked stroking her daughter's hair. She had lovely hair, long and straight and blonde. Like Mary in Peter, Paul and Mary.

'You know what Cliff phoned to say?'

'What?' asked Peg.

'That he still loves her! What kind of twisted mind game is he playing?'

'Maybe he does love her.'

'Are you kidding? While he's boinking some dude? Give me a break! He's messing with her head. That's what guys do.'

Peg studied the girl's profile in the dim television light. A face soft with youth, but hard with certainty. 'You're so sure? About what guys do.'

'Well yeah.' She seemed surprised by the question.

'How?'

'Remember after Dad left? *It's you and me against the world*, you used to say.'

'That was a long time ago.'

'But that's how it is. You can't count on any of them.'

That was also a direct quote: Peg, circa 1969. She had been listening. Her little girl.

Things had moved on a bit since then. Times were different. Peg was different.

Mary Denise was repeating Peg's own slogans from ten years ago.

Aww, don't take it to heart. Mary Denise doesn't like anybody.

The commercial ended. With a musical fanfare the film returned.

'Oh, remember this part? This is the good part,' said Mary Denise. She slumped down into her seat.

Sadness seeped into Peg, heavy tides of it lapping at her heart, her bones. 'I love this part,' she said. She sat down on the couch next to her daughter and they watched the rest of the movie.

LENNON AND MCCARTNEY

HE USED TO LOVE my boobs. At the start when we would stay in bed all weekend. *Just the four of us*, he'd say; *you, me and the boobs.* He loved them so much he named them—Lennon and McCartney. Reading left to right. Our first flat had a big bed, high, because there were three old mattresses piled on top of the box spring. Each was thin, but together they were like a big cloud that gathered us, cuddled us together. We had this floaty pink duvet and about a hundred little pillows and we'd just be in there forever; Dave on top, then me on top, then pretzeled into some Kama Sutra position from the books he bought us. On and on, until we were red and raw and sweaty and giggly. Our cat Peanut would try to sit on my belly but I'd be laughing too hard. My stomach rolled like ocean waves. She'd give up, find a little nook between our bodies and snuggle in, soft and warm.

Now Dave keeps saying to me, *remember the old days?* I do, of course I do. What he's really asking is why don't we spend weekends in bed anymore? We have a proper bed now, in a proper house. He thinks I've gone off him. That he's lost too much hair, gained too much gut. I try to reassure him. Okay, he looks different, but who doesn't? Lennon and McCartney have lost some of their perk. He says *nah, still perfect.* But he doesn't really think so. He doesn't paw at them like he used to. Sometimes when we're getting ready to go out I'll ask him about my outfit, my hair, and he'll say *fine, fine.* But he's got his back to me. He doesn't even look.

I tell Dave the problem is the weather. This country has about the least sexy weather. The rain in winter; the cold in your bones, the sky always leaning on you. No light. The wind off the river that wants to strip off your skin, and no matter which way you're going you're always walking into it. Somehow it's never at your back.

He says the weather hasn't changed since we first got married. He's very logical, very exact. It gets tiring. I say no, I know that. Although there is global warming. He says, now we're not having sex because of global warming? I didn't mean that, I say. I meant that I don't feel sexy when I'm shivering and my hair is dripping wet. And I'm tired. And I know this isn't possible, but when I remember us in the Lennon and McCartney phase it's always a bright blue and gold day in mid-September. Sun. Smell of cut grass through the open window. Heat.

Now it's November. The Christmas lights aren't up over Shop Street yet. It's too soon to have my class making ornaments. Too early to start talking to them about how Christmas is a festival of light in the darkest part of the year. Such a dark year. Bombs in the London Underground, a hurricane in New Orleans. They know about all these things, they ask about them; it's hard to know what to say. You can't protect them from the mess of the world. Though I still try. Glitter, glue and festivals of light. Not yet, though. We're still in the time before the light.

I'm not sure why we've never had children.

Dave says first we had no money and now we have no time. He says we need to talk about that. Make a definite decision one way or the other.

I'm taking this class at night. Human Resource Management. We thought that if I ever want to try for Assistant Principal it'd be a good credit to have. Dave works crazy hours these days, the housing boom has been great for his firm, so I'm on my own sometimes in the evening. I'd first wanted to do French. I'm not sure why. But we discussed it and decided it was better to invest in my career, my future.

The class is only okay. A lot of it is simply fancy words for ideas that are pure common sense. But I enjoy the bus ride there and back. I like having the time to think. It's all doing these days, so sitting still and thinking is a luxury.

Last Thursday, though, I wasn't even thinking. Too tired. I get really tired. And especially on the way home, my brain just stuffed with HR terminology. So I was staring out the window. Which is a funny thing to do when it's dark outside and the bus is all lit-up inside. It's all reflections. And then I saw this thing that was so strange, it made me feel cold all over. We were passing the Bohermore Cemetery. Across the road there's a bridal shop with a row of mannequins in wedding dresses in its window. Big white gauzy wedding dresses. The window stays lit even when the shop is closed. So I was looking out at the cemetery, the pale elaborate gravestones marking the moonlit hill. One tree that looked like its head was bent in sorrow. And then I saw wedding dresses. Reflected, ghost-white, in a row among the graves. Like they were queuing for something. Maybe some ritual. Maybe a dance.

A trick of the light, Dave would say. If I told him. But I'm not going to. To me it was like a dream, only I've rarely felt wider awake. Brides in a graveyard—it's the whole script, isn't it? With all the other stuff we fill our hours with missing. Take away work and taxes and the dishwasher's hum and what-will-I-make-for-dinner. And whose parents should we spend Christmas with, and errands and HR and under-arm deodorant. And recycling and did the car pass its NCT? As we shuffle inexorably from marriage rites to burial rites, all that stuff is just distraction. Glitter and glue.

The bus went speeding down the hill. We hurtled past houses dark with curtains drawn, hunched in on themselves, the weak blue light of televisions like a faint pulse. And then the Square. Traffic, streetlamps, college-age clubbers crossing against the light, horns honking, laughter. Slouching, loud, indestructible children; this late they own the Square. I stepped down into the midst of them.

It was colder off the bus but the wind beat at me like vast wings and there was something good in that. The wind and the footsteps and voices and trees swaying. Usually I just change busses at the Square. But this time it occurred to me I didn't have to. I didn't have to do anything, I could do what I liked. I stood there thinking and the next thing my legs were carrying me forward toward that big hotel. The old Great Southern. I crossed the street and went right up the stone steps and in through the heavy revolving door. Black and white tile in the foyer. I went straight to the fireplace.

'I bring you something?' There was something so kind in the way she said it, as though she really hoped I'd answer yes. I'd only ever been inside to use the loo. A distant piano began to play, something twinkly, jazzy. A woman laughed, somewhere. The Polish woman smiled. 'Can I bring you something to drink?' In the firelight her face was soft gold.

'I'm...just getting warm.' I wanted to be invisible.

She nodded. 'Brandy? Is warm.'

And I said, 'Okay.' Even though I don't drink brandy, except sometimes at Christmas. But now I felt like I was a character in a film, and this character drank brandy. It was like that, I was sort of watching myself from a distance.

The Polish waitress smiled again and gestured to the fat black couch under the window. 'Please, sit. I bring your brandy.' And she went out the doorway and turned right. I took off my coat and folded myself onto the couch, which was very low. I wasn't too graceful about it. But the couch was sort of velvety and it felt nice to sit down. I took out my mobile and sent Dave a text. *Will be late.* That was all I could think of to say. Then I did something really strange. I kicked off my shoes and stretched my legs so my feet could feel the fire. I wiggled my toes. It felt just wonderful.

The waitress came back. She saw me with my feet sticking out and giggled. But it was a nice giggle, very girly, and I giggled too.

She set a brandy down on the table in front of me, slipping a red serviette underneath it. When she leaned over I could see her boobs. They were high and round and just held by the white lace bra she wore beneath her blouse. They were young. *Rubber Soul* boobs. Mine were *Let It Be* and already thinking about solo careers.

I said, 'Thank you,' and she walked away. I made a point of not checking out her backside. The brandy was that old photograph colour and it moved like oil when I tipped the glass. The smell was exquisite. I took a small sip and it was pure heat in my mouth, my throat. I sighed.

I stood to check how I looked in the mirror above the fireplace. My reflection surprised me. I looked different. My eyes were bright, my cheeks flushed. I reapplied lip gloss. Okay. Not too bad. My hair was a mess so I took it down and brushed it, hard. It felt good. When I finished it lay across my shoulders and sort of glimmered in the firelight.

I stood on tiptoe to check out my cleavage. Huh. I thought that after all there were some pretty good songs on *Let It Be*. The woman in the mirror grinned at me.

I was the film character again. Woman smiling in hotel lobby. What would she do next? And when was the last time I didn't know what I would do next? Whole seasons, whole years of planning in my rear-view mirror. Schedules and checklists. When was the last time I surprised myself?

Next semester, French. To hell with HR. French, certainement.

I sat back down, put my hairbrush and lip gloss away in my bag. My bag was black. My shoes and trousers were black. My jumper was grey. Needed something. A red scarf.

I drank more brandy. Je voudrais une something rouge. What was French for scarf? Je voudrais—I would like...

My phone beeped. Dave.

How late is late? He didn't ask what was keeping me.

I texted back. *Why don't you ask if I'm ok?*

Are you ok?

Yes. Fine.

So when will you be home?

Present tense of je voudrais...what was it? I want. I want.

Don't know. I want not to know.

Drank more brandy. Just a trickle left.

Beep. *What are you doing?*

Why do you need to know? As soon as I sent it I felt bad. But I was annoyed.

There was a long pause in which I drained my glass. Then his answer came.

Cos I miss you.

Dave. Oh, Dave.

And then I had a thought. In all our years together I'd never settled on a word for Dave's penis. *Dick, cock, willie.* None of the usual words were fond enough. But suddenly I knew the pet name he would really, really like. I responded.

Come to me. My hand was trembling.

WHERE ARE YOU?

Hotel. Great Southern. I want you. Dave, I want you. My face and neck went hot.

You've lost it!

Don't argue. I'm booking a room.

Long pause. Then: *Use the Visa. Mastercard is full.*

Okay.

What's got into you?

I almost couldn't type out the words. I mean, this wasn't me. I'd never done anything like this. I was the woman in the film now.

I want your lips on Lennon and McCartney. I want to feel your Clapton inside me.

I thought about waiting for his response. But I didn't. Instead I turned off my phone.

Then the woman in the film smiled, put on her shoes and walked to the front desk.